DINOSAUR

B L A C K O U T

DINOSAUR
B L A C K O U T

JUDITH SILVERTHORNE

Edited by Barbara Sapergia.
Cover illustrations by Aries Cheung.
Cover and book design by Duncan Campbell.
Printed and bound in Canada at Gauvin Press.
This book is printed on 100% recycled paper.

Mixed Sources
Product group from well-managed forests and recycled wood or fiber
www.fsc.org Cert no. SGS-COC-2624
© 1996 Forest Stewardship Council

National Library of Canada Cataloguing in Publication Data

Silverthorne, Judith, date-
      Dinosaur blackout / Judith Silverthorne.

(Dinosaur adventure series ; 4)
Includes bibliographical references.
ISBN 978-1-55050-375-3

1. Dinosaurs—Juvenile fiction. I. Title. II. Series: Silverthorne, Judith, 1953—Dinosaur adventure series ; 4.
PS8587.I2763D545 2008   jC813'.54   C2008-900241-5

10 9 8 7 6 5 4 3 2 1

COTEAU
BOOKS
FOR KIDS

2517 Victoria Ave
Regina, Saskatchewan
Canada S4P OT2

available in Canada and the US from:
Fitzhenry & Whiteside
195 Allstate Parkway
Markham, Ontario
Canada L3R 4T8

The publisher gratefully acknowledges the financial assistance of the Saskatchewan Arts Board, the Canada Council for the Arts, including the Millennium Arts Fund, the Government of Canada through the Book Publishing Industry Development Program (BPIDP), Association for the Export of Canadian Books, and the City of Regina Arts Commission, for its publishing program.

SASKATCHEWAN
ARTS BOARD

Canada Council   Conseil des
for the Arts   Arts du Canada

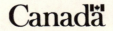
Canada

Regina
CITY OF REGINA

As always, to my son, Aaron,
who inspired me with this series
from the beginning.

To Modeste McKenzie,
many thanks for the imaginative details
in the final venture to the past.

And to Susan McKenzie
for suggestions throughout.

CHAPTER ONE

Daniel awoke with a niggling feeling in the pit of his stomach. He couldn't remember his dreams, just a feeling of unease and the memory of a strange sound that ran through them. As he dressed, he noted how the low angles of late summer sunlight glinted off his computer, highlighting the rows of books and dinosaur replicas on the shelves above his desk. He could hear the *fee-bee-bee* of chickadees chattering in the caragana hedge below his open window. And downstairs Mom rattled pans and dishes as she made breakfast. The aroma of coffee and sizzling sausages wafted upwards. His two-year-old sister Cheryl must still be sleeping. He didn't hear her usual chatter. Everything seemed normal and he couldn't figure out what was bothering him.

Dad was sure to be halfway down the valley at the farm's campsite, seeing if the tourists needed any help preparing for one of the day's tours. At an excavation not far from the campsite, visitors could see a real dinosaur dig and even help with work on a small sample plot. If anything were wrong there, Dad would be sure to come to the house for help. The operation was simple though, and aside from guests having mechanical difficulties with their campers, there was little that could go wrong. Daniel and his best friend Jed Lindstrom had checked the night before that there was ample water and firewood. They'd fed and pastured the trail-ride horses and made sure the campfires were doused.

But the uneasiness persisted as Daniel headed to the barn, only slipping to the back of his mind as he carried out his chores. While he milked Daisy, he studied how the bright shaft of sunlight from the high windows outlined the mangers and stalls of the old wooden barn with its packed dirt floor and wall ladder that led to the hayloft.

When Craig and Todd Nelwin rattled open the big sliding door some time later, light streamed in and the dust motes danced down the centre corridor. Marble's kittens skittered about, playing with pieces of straw that fluttered to the ground like butterflies each time a puff of fresh autumn air swept through the barn.

The brothers had been working at the Bringhams' all summer, as restitution for bullying attacks on Daniel and vandalism at the campsite. They'd been better workers than anyone expected, and after their debt was paid, Daniel's father had hired them for the rest of the summer.

The boys lived alone with an abusive father – their mother had died five years ago. Now they were almost like part of Daniel's family. Craig had even developed an interest in dinosaurs.

Daniel snorted back a laugh as he caught sight of Craig. The younger brother's light brown hair stuck out in all directions, like a windmill gone wonky. Obviously the stocky fifteen-year-old had not taken the time to plaster it down as he usually did. In contrast, sixteen-year-old Todd's dark bristly hair stood on end all the time, though it seemed to spike to attention even more this morning, like a frightened porcupine. But neither boy had any fresh bruises to indicate that their father might be hitting them again.

Daniel supposed that with the boys working at his family's place full-time, their dad didn't have time to harass his sons. Horace Nelwin seemed to have accepted them working away from home, though he insisted they do their chores at home, morning and night. His mean streak flared whenever they were late.

"What're we doing at the quarry today?" Craig asked, grabbing a pitchfork from a nail on the wall and starting to clean the stalls.

"Nothing special that I know of," Daniel replied. He expected that they'd continue uncovering the *Stygimoloch* skeleton they'd been working on for the past couple of months. Mr. Pederson, their neighbour and Daniel's friend, had discovered the skeleton of the fairly rare plant-eating dinosaur. Sometimes referred to as "thorny devils" or "demons from the river Styx," the small pachycephalosaurs had bumpy skulls rimmed with many one-hundred millimetre horns. Pederson and Daniel had been exploring the fossil sites for a year and a half now, and the *Stygimoloch* was one of their most exciting discoveries.

Craig shook his head in disappointment. "Too bad we couldn't go prospecting," he said. Prospecting meant looking for places that might contain fossils, and Mr. Pederson had promised to show them how to do it.

Daniel thought about it. "You know, after this weekend, there aren't any visitors scheduled for quarry tours. Maybe we could talk Mr. Pederson into going next week."

"We'll have to do it soon. School starts on Thursday," Craig reminded him, leaning on the fork.

Todd spoke up. "I'd like to go too."

"You would?" asked Daniel, trying not to look too surprised. Todd had never shown an interest in the time-consuming work of uncovering dinosaurs before.

Todd shrugged. "Sure, why not?"

"'Cause you always prefer to help Daniel's dad with the farm work, rather than digging at the quarry," Craig said.

"Doesn't mean I can't be interested in paleontology too." Todd nudged his brother with a muscular shoulder. He looked a bit embarrassed, but determined.

"Guess not." Craig regained his balance.

Daniel agreed. "No problem. We'll ask Mr. Pederson this morning then."

"Great." Todd swung the pitchfork around and began scooping up the manure in the first stall. Craig set to work, whistling.

As usual, the brothers worked in tandem, with Todd taking the lead and Craig following behind. This morning they made a game of their chores, challenging one another to see whose energy would give out first at the fastest pace they could go. Loading pitchforks with manure and heaping it onto the stoneboat for later removal, then chucking bales of hay and spreading the clean straw around the stall was strenuous work. They were soon sweating and grunting.

Daniel watched the pair, listening to the sounds of the barn – the *squirt*, *squirt* of milk hitting the metal pail, several lazy flies buzzing and cows rustling in the straw bedding at their feet. But when he grew bored with the boys' antics, Daniel felt anxiety rising to the surface of his mind again.

Shuffling the playful kittens out from under his feet, Daniel moved over to milk Lily, then carried the pails of milk to the separating room. As he released the cows into the fenced pasture for the day, his golden retriever appeared from over the rise of a hill and scampered towards the barn.

"Dactyl, how're you doing, boy?" Daniel bent to scratch behind the dog's ears, continuing down his back, burrowing his hands into the thick, furry coat. Daniel had named him after the prehistoric *Pterodactyls* that had once flown through these very skies.

Dactyl lifted a paw for a handshake and waited for a treat. Daniel pulled a small biscuit out of his pocket. Dactyl rose on his hind legs with a little whining noise in his throat and Daniel popped a tasty morsel into the dog's mouth. With a few quick chomps, it was gone.

Daniel continued to pat his dog, gazing out at the rolling hills of southwest Saskatchewan and the Frenchman River Valley. Several miles to the south of the Bringham farm lay the town of Climax. To the east was the town of Eastend with its T. rex Discovery Centre and the Royal Saskatchewan Museum field station. Although the entire area looked scrubby and uninteresting to some eyes, Daniel knew the terrain concealed many treasures in the form of prehistoric fossils. The coulees and buttes also camouflaged the homes of antelope, mule deer and black-tailed prairie dogs. To Daniel, it was the best place he could imagine.

Daniel scanned the valley below, where his secret hideout lay in a gully, its opening hidden by brush to keep away prying eyes. He had no sense of concern when he thought about his collections of fossils, rocks and paleon-tological gear stashed inside. Although several people, including his parents, his neighbour Ole Pederson and Dr. Mildred Roost – a visiting paleontologist – knew of its location, they had no reason to intrude.

Nor did the Nelwin brothers, at least not since they'd trashed the place earlier in the summer and had to clean it up. Besides, they were too busy concentrating on the finds at the quarry and assisting the guests who came to explore. And they still had to keep up with the farm work.

But the feeling of disquiet arose again. Something wasn't right. Daniel tried to shake it off as he saw Dad walk into the yard.

"Wait up!" he called. He and Dactyl raced over and they all walked to the house together.

"Things okay down there?" Daniel indicated the campsite.

"Sure," Dad answered. "Why do you ask?"

"No reason," he said, breathing a sigh of relief. As they chatted, Daniel scanned the cloudless sky. No indication of bad weather brewing.

By the time he and Dad washed and returned to the kitchen, the Nelwins had arrived and seated themselves at their customary spots at the breakfast table. His sister Cheryl sat in her high chair, squishing bits of pancake in chokecherry syrup, then stuffing them into her mouth with contented little murmurs. Bits of purple streaked the fluffy blonde curls around her face.

Moments later, the sound of crunching gravel in their driveway meant Ole Pederson had arrived. A tap on the door, followed by its swift opening, revealed him and Dr. Mildred Roost. Mom greeted them warmly. Mildred Roost removed her Tilley hat, letting it dangle down her back on its wind cord, revealing her long, braided grey hair. She stamped her metal cane along the floor, even though she didn't really need it, taking a chair closest to the door. Mr. Pederson chose the seat beside her, curling his long legs beneath his chair.

"Good morning!" Dad slid into his place at the head of the table, beaming at everyone.

"Hard to believe summer is about over," Dr. Roost sighed, shifting her cane to a more comfortable position on the back of her chair.

"Yes, and our first tourist season has almost come to an end too," said Mom, serving their pancakes with a flourish.

Ole Pederson's grey-blue eyes twinkled as he patted the wisps of grey hair in place over his forehead to hide his receding hairline. "I'd say in many ways it's been quite a success!"

Everyone chorused an agreement. All their long hours to prepare the dig and construct a campsite had created a new attraction in the area. The many tours they'd given had worked well.

"After this Labour Day long weekend, we'll have to tally up the final financial results," Dad said, reaching for the syrup.

Ole Pederson nodded. "Yes, that's what'll help us decide if we want to do it again next year."

"And if the bank will give us the go-ahead," added Mom.

Daniel sat up with a jolt. He'd never even considered that they wouldn't continue. All he could think about was how important their discoveries were to the paleontology world, how exciting it was to learn about prehistoric times.

"But we've had plenty of people coming for the tours," Daniel spluttered.

"Yes," Dad agreed, "but that doesn't mean we've made enough money at it to support us all."

Two families, Daniel's and his friend Jed's, along with Ole Pederson, operated the paleontology dig and campground for tourists interested in learning more about dinosaurs and the world they lived in. They'd planned the venture as a way of providing extra income to keep their farms alive. And Ole Pederson was the centre of it all. He'd discovered the skeleton of an *Edmontosaurus* almost two years earlier and he'd also helped establish a dinosaur museum in Climax. Daniel had been involved with Mr. Pederson in the preparation of the bones.

"The sooner we discuss the future, the better," agreed Mr. Pederson. "Especially now that we've found the *Stygimoloch* and there are indications of other possible finds."

"As soon as we release the information about the *Stygimoloch*, we'll have even more visitors," Daniel suggested. Until Daniel and Pederson found their almost whole skeleton, there had only been five partial skulls found in North America and those had been discovered in Montana and Wyoming in 1983.

"Yes, but we're still not quite ready to do that," Dad said.

"Indeed," Ole Pederson added, "we need to finish retrieving the entire fossil and verify it as much as possible. I want to make sure we do this right."

Dr. Roost snorted, "Yeah, and that nosy news reporter from Eastend, Adrian McDermott, is already suspicious that we have something special here."

"He's just looking for any kind of news to fill up the paper," Mom said. "He's young, he's fresh out of journalism school and he's excited..."

"And he's a pain," said Ole Pederson.

"Yeah, but it's got to be tough for him when nothing exciting goes on in this area otherwise," Dad said.

"Just seems like he's everywhere. But I suppose he does cover every bake sale and school event, which is important to people around here," Mr. Pederson admitted.

"And the story he did on our tourist operation last month brought more people our way," said Daniel. "Maybe if we had more publicity, we'd have even more people coming and we'd be sure of being able to continue."

"You might be right, Daniel," said Dad, "but still we'll have to wait and see how things go and do them in the right order. We don't want to jeopardize Mr. Pederson's work and reveal anything before we're ready."

"At least when the time is right to get it into the news, you know he'll be a good one to go to," Dr. Roost said, chuckling.

Daniel sighed to himself. He sure hoped they'd be able to continue the tourism operation the following year and, of course, keep the farm. He had the best of all worlds right now, living the rural life and being able to dig for dinosaur bones. But the greatest part of the last couple of years had been his astonishing excursions into prehistoric time. He had been flung into the world of late Cretaceous Period dinosaurs – the very paleontological age they were unearthing in their quarry.

Although the first couple of trips happened by accident, his last terrifying adventure was one he'd planned. He'd meant to go alone, but Dr. Roost had turned up at the last minute and insisted on coming along. The adventure had almost cost them their lives.

Now, even though Daniel knew a way to go back to the past again, it wasn't something he wanted to attempt for a good long time. He had safely hidden some prehistoric foliage that could transport him back. Pederson and Dr. Roost knew nothing about it, but he was pretty sure Craig knew that there was still a way to go back.

As the conversation bubbled around him, Daniel concentrated on the delicious whole wheat saskatoon berry pancakes smothered in plain yogurt and drizzled with tangy-sweet chokecherry syrup, followed with bites of spicy homemade sausage. He noticed the Nelwins digging in with relish too. At last, he had his fill, and washed the meal down with a final refreshing jolt of freshly squeezed orange juice.

"Terrific, as usual, Libby," Ole Pederson told Daniel's mom, patting his stomach. As Pederson shoved back his chair and reached for his hat, Dr. Roost nodded in agreement, swallowing the last of her coffee.

"Ready to head out?" she asked.

Pederson nodded. "I want to get an early start." He looked at Daniel and Craig. "You boys ready?"

"Sure," they chorused.

Pederson turned to Todd. "You staying here or coming with us?"

Todd looked at Daniel's dad. "We have the west field to finish harvesting, right?"

Dad gave Todd an understanding smile. "Yes, though if you wanted to go with them this morning, you could. The crop is so poor, it won't take long to finish it."

"No, that's fine. I'll stay here." But Daniel thought he saw Todd's disappointment.

Everyone rose and moved at once, taking their dishes to the sink, then heading for the door and their various tasks. The Lindstrom family would arrive soon and Jed would conduct the first tour and join the quarry group later to work on his special project. His sister Lucy would take the first trail-ride group. As usual, Jed's dad, Doug Lindstrom, would help Dad at the camp and on the farm, while his mom, Greta, supervised the outdoor kitchen operation with Daniel's mom. Jed's other two sisters, Leanne and Lindsay, would help prepare meals and babysit Cheryl.

Daniel fed leftovers to Dactyl and added some crunchy dog food to his bowl. He refilled his pet's water dish, and then swung his backpack over his shoulder and joined the others at the edge of the yard. As they headed across the pasture, Daniel walked with Mr. Pederson. Dr. Roost and Craig poked along behind them, chatting. Above them, a hawk swooped down the valley, with a harsh *keeer* cry. Gophers dashed into holes in front of them with warning squeaks, their stubby tails flipping out of sight.

Around them, the fading landscape signalled the end of summer. Velvety goldenrod and scarlet paintbrush dotted the thick, yellowing grass and drying scrub. Canada thistle and sage had gone to seed and brown ragweed sprang up here and there. The last sweet smell of clover growing along the ditches filled the crisp air, along with the scents of harvesting in the fields beyond. Geese were beginning to gather for their long journey south, snacking on bits of grain the combines had left behind.

As they walked across the gently sloping hills to the quarry, Pederson seemed to have a constant tickle in his throat. Each time he coughed, Daniel's stomach gave a little lurch. Was *this* what was worrying him – that Mr. Pederson hadn't been looking well lately?

"You're not catching a cold, are you?" Daniel asked, keeping up with the old man's long strides. He worried that it might turn into something worse.

Pederson shook his head. "No. It's just the grain dust from the harvesting."

Daniel looked up at the slight haze in the sky. He could hear the distant roar of tractors, combines and grain trucks from several directions. "You've never had allergies before, have you?"

"There's a first time for everything," Pederson continued. "Seems to be more dust than usual. Guess it's because it's been such a dry year and there's more chaff than grain in the crops."

"Are you sure that's all it is?" Daniel asked, though he knew crops were so poor that some farmers hadn't even bothered to harvest.

Pederson kept his eyes straight ahead. "When a fellow gets as old as I am, the body just acts up sometimes."

Daniel protested, "No way! You're not old."

Pederson chuckled. "I've been old for a long time."

Daniel stared at his friend, recalling when they'd first met, and had to admit that Mr. Pederson had been old even then. But Daniel never really thought about what that meant or that Pederson might be gone someday. He was still so agile and quick-witted. Then Daniel recalled that his Grandfather Bringham had been about the same age when he died several years earlier.

A chill ran up Daniel's body as he recalled Pederson's bout with pneumonia during a snowstorm two winters earlier. Daniel had been terrified, but Ole had recovered with the help of Daniel's family. Since then, he'd had the occasional attack of bronchitis in the cold spells, but his coughing now was a little disconcerting.

"Nothing to worry about, lad," Pederson patted his shoulder.

Daniel suddenly remembered the question he meant to ask. "Do you think we could go on a prospecting trip after the weekend?"

Pederson contemplated for a moment. "I don't see why not."

"Craig and Todd want to come too."

Pederson smiled. "Yes, I did promise to take them, and Jed too. And Mildred will probably enjoy it. In fact, we should see who else would like to go. The more sharp eyes, the better."

"School starts Thursday, though, so could we go before that?" Daniel asked.

"How about Monday morning, bright and early, seeing as how Sunday is our last official tour day?" Pederson's eyes twinkled.

Daniel kicked at a clod of grass and whooped. The thought of what fossils might lie hidden only a few metres below their feet gave him goosebumps. Who knew what they might uncover?

"Hey, Craig!" he turned back to the pair behind them. "We're going prospecting on Monday."

"Yes!" Craig grinned, before turning excitedly to Dr. Roost to see what she had to say about it.

"In the meantime, let's see how much work we can get done over the next few days to secure what we've already found," suggested Pederson.

Daniel quickened his pace. "Sure thing!"

Pederson speeded up too, and when they looked back, Dr. Roost and Craig weren't far behind them. Every time Daniel and Pederson sped up, the others did too, until they were almost running. They could hear the others laughing behind them.

Moments later and out of breath, Daniel and Pederson cleared the last hilltop before the quarry and made their way down the various cutaways and ledges that took them to the roped-off areas, each a separate work site with its own special finds. Immediately below the next overhang was the *Stygimoloch* skeleton. Daniel leapt down, then stopped short.

"No!" he shouted.

Pederson caught up and let out a shriek of disbelief.

"What's wrong?" Craig asked as he and Dr. Roost appeared moments later. They too stood with their mouths wide open, gaping at the empty hole at their feet.

The *Stygimoloch* skeleton was gone!

"Great snakes and blasted lizards!" Mildred Roost yowled.

Ole Pederson coughed several times, looking ready to collapse. Craig guided him down to a ledge where he sat, his face pinched with shock.

The night before, several sections of the small dinosaur – which was about the size of an ostrich – had been swathed in heavy field jackets on the edge of the six-metre long by five-metre wide cavity. The pieces were ready for transport to the lab at the Royal Saskatchewan Museum field station at Eastend. Now those, along with every last one of the bones they'd exposed over the last few weeks, had vanished.

The once carefully dug excavation was now a shambles, with crude gashes where the last of the fossils had lain. Scuffle marks were everywhere and their tools scattered.

To start the dig, they'd used a backhoe to remove the top chunk of the hill and then shovels to cut steps into the hillside like a huge set of stairs down to the fossil bed. Each step was about a metre square and about thirty centimetres high. Their most recent work had involved digging out the back end of the skeleton, which had been buried in heavy soil. Daniel and Mr. Pederson had spent hours with garden trowels and paint brushes to reveal the intricate tailbone. They'd even found an imprint of the scaly, reptilian dinosaur skin.

"Who on earth would do such an atrocious thing?" Dr. Roost leaned heavily on her cane. The others shook their heads.

Daniel knelt and let the earth run through his fingers, searching for bits of fossils of any kind, but came up empty-handed. Someone had trampled and scattered the small mounds of dirt they'd left the day before. They'd planned to sift through them later, but that wasn't possible now. He swallowed hard, trying to gulp back the bowling ball-sized lump that seemed lodged in his throat.

Pederson still sat on his ledge, his face buried in his hands.

Now Daniel knew why he'd been so on edge. This dig meant everything to him and Pederson, and maybe to the others as well. He'd worried about leaving it unguarded at night, but it seemed silly to think anything would happen. Now his forebodings had become reality!

He remembered waking up and thinking he'd heard something strange in the night. Now he knew it was true.

CHAPTER TWO

"**T**his ruins everything!" Craig spoke at last.

Dr. Roost stirred. "No way," she growled. "We'll find the bloody culprits."

"Maybe," said Daniel. "Look. Tire tracks."

Craig joined him and the two followed the tracks for a few metres. "All-terrain vehicles, I think."

Studying the ground, Daniel agreed. He and Craig walked some distance along the quarry, but the ATV tracks disappeared into the scrub.

Pederson rose at last. "Let's call in the authorities. They'll have a better chance of following the trail." He pulled out a cell phone and handed it to Daniel. "Here, you know how to use this contraption. Dial your folks for me."

Daniel obliged and Ole Pederson explained the situation to Ed Bringham with a request to contact Corporal Jim Fraser at the Climax RCMP detachment.

"Use the west roadway when you come," Pederson suggested. "The thieves seem to have come and gone to the east and we don't want to mess up the trail."

"Tell them to bring my camera too," Daniel whispered to Pederson.

"Better yet, they could bring my digital," suggested Dr. Roost, not bothering to lower her voice. "It's in my truck. My spare keys are under the rear bumper."

Pederson relayed the instructions and then his face dropped again. "Yes, the lot of us are mighty upset," he said. He listened some more. "Yes, we'll come up with a contingency plan."

Pederson ended the call and turned to Daniel. "Jed left with his group only a few minutes behind us. They gathered early."

"Oh, no! They'll be here any minute," said Daniel, shaking his head. "What'll we do?"

Dr. Roost took charge of the situation. "Do the usual micro and macro displays. Ole, you up for that or shall I do the explanations?"

"No use whining about what's happened, I guess," he said. He massaged his wrinkled forehead with his fingers as if to ease a headache.

"Good." She turned and pointed her cane at Craig. "You can explain about the cutting of the steps and layers of earth to get down to the fossils. Daniel, you run and meet Jed and have him direct the group to his own area first."

Daniel nodded. Jed would be pleased. Usually his area was off limits to visitors because of the fragility of the find.

He'd discovered rare tiny scratching marks of a birdlike creature. They were still trying to figure out its origins.

Mildred Roost continued. "I'll watch for Ed and Corporal Fraser and direct them away from the tour group."

"Wait a minute," Daniel stopped in his tracks. "We don't know what condition the rest of the site is in."

"That's right," said Dr. Roost. "Craig, run and see if there's anything left over there. Wave if it's fine."

A shrill whistle pierced the air. The pre-arranged signal warned them of the tour group's imminent arrival. Daniel rushed off.

"Watch for Craig's wave," Dr. Roost called after him.

Daniel took off over the rise and met the tour group just on the other side. Jed looked puzzled, but Daniel shook his head slightly so he wouldn't say anything.

"Welcome to the quarry," said Daniel. "As Jed's probably told you, we've made some interesting discoveries here this summer." He stalled with general comments, watching for Craig. When he spotted the all-clear signal, he continued walking. "This morning we have a special treat for you. You're going to see a rare find discovered by your guide, Jed."

The four adults and two young boys seemed pleased. Jed still looked puzzled.

"First, if you'd like to step over this way, you'll get a good view of the valley and quarry before we go down." He led them to the top of the rise.

While the group was busy examining the view and snapping pictures, Daniel pulled Jed aside. "I can't tell you everything right now, but you have to avoid going anywhere near the *Stygimoloch* site. Keep them busy with the micro and macro sites, and then take them the long way around to your special markings, and back to the farm."

"What's happened?" Jed kept his voice low.

Daniel pressed Jed's arm and spoke softly. "The *Stygimoloch* bones have been stolen."

"What?" Jed gasped. "Who could have done such a thing?"

"I have no idea. We just discovered it."

Jed looked shocked.

"We've called Corporal Fraser, but we don't know when he'll get here." Daniel gripped Jed's arm. "Can you carry on? Pretend everything's okay?"

Jed cleared his throat, swallowed hard, and then joined the sightseers. He explained that the different terms used at the site as he led the group towards Craig.

Who would steal the *Stygimoloch* and what did they intend on doing with it?

Daniel stumbled back into the quarry in search of Dr. Roost. She stood guard over the empty *Stygimoloch* site, looking more upset than ever.

"Is something else wrong?" Daniel rushed to her side.

Dr. Roost eyed Daniel for a moment before replying. "No, this is bad enough. I just can't figure out who would have done it. It doesn't make sense."

"Could it be someone trying to get the credit for uncovering something new?"

She shook her head. "I've thought about that, but I can't see anyone being able to pull it off. You and Ole have documented everything so well, including with photographs, and you've shown your findings and pictures to people at the Royal Saskatchewan Museum, so it would be exceptionally difficult for anyone to claim the find as theirs. Besides, I don't think people on the tours realized what they were seeing."

"But what other reason could there be?" Daniel heard his voice crack with exasperation.

"Sabotage!" Dr. Roost looked grim again.

Daniel gulped.

Dr. Roost pointed with her cane. "Take a look at those tread marks. No one with any sense or knowledge about paleontology would be so careless with something so valuable."

"An 'outside' job?" Daniel speculated.

A smile threatened to crack Dr. Roost's face.

"You could say that."

"Or maybe it's an insider, making it look like an outside job."

Dr. Roost guffawed at Daniel's remark. "You've been watching too much TV! All this talk about insiders and outside jobs."

"Well, it is possible isn't it?" Daniel asked.

"Yes, it certainly is!" She pointed to a mound of earth that lay untouched. "But who on the 'inside' would do such a thing? We're all part of the operation. Its success benefits for all of us."

"True." But Daniel's mind flashed over the trouble he'd had with the Nelwin brothers earlier this summer. They had bullied him and damaged his hideout and the campsite. He shook the thought off. Craig and Todd had worked hard to make things right, and he couldn't believe either of them would be involved after all his family had done for them.

Dr. Roost looked at him with curiosity. "You have an idea?"

Daniel shook his head.

"And what do you make of that?" Dr. Roost pointed to a section a little farther off where they'd started clearing some debris to expose tiny bones.

He started to head over to it, but Mildred Roost caught his arm. "Best leave it until after the police have had a chance to look at it and we've taken some photographs."

Daniel squatted and peered at the mound from a distance. "I think whoever trashed the place just took what was easy. I don't think they know that they'll never be able to sell them."

"I agree," said Ole Pederson, coming up behind him. "Even if they eventually found some disreputable group to buy them, it would be years before they could allow them to surface, and that doesn't make any sense."

"Since when did stealing ever make sense?" asked Dr. Roost, snorting. "Is the tour group gone?"

Pederson nodded. "Thanks for distracting me earlier, Mildred. I'm calmer now."

"Action in crisis is always the best," she answered, lifting her eyebrows. "So how do you think we should proceed once the police have gone?"

Pederson stood with his hand under his chin, surveying the damage. "Guess that'll depend on when we get any news about our *Stygimoloch*. The work on it has been seriously compromised. Who's to say what condition the bones will be in, when and if we find them?" Pederson sighed and his eyes held a faraway look.

Everyone stood lost in thought.

"Well, there's still Jed's splendid discovery to finish collecting," Dr. Roost stated quietly. "Those little markings could be an exceptional find!"

Pederson gave her a weak smile, but his shoulders drooped and he seemed frailer than Daniel ever remembered him being.

"We'll get the fossils back," Daniel said, patting Mr. Pederson's hand, but he wasn't so sure himself.

Daniel was relieved to hear the sounds of a vehicle coming their way across the pasture. Craig joined them and they all watched in silence as Doug Lindstrom's old jeep stopped at the top of the hill. Corporal Fraser got out, along with Dad and Doug, and they all came down the steps to the quarry.

Doug let out a low whistle of disbelief. Dad's lips

clamped tight. Corporal Fraser looked grim as he surveyed the destruction.

"They were thorough, I will say that for them," the police officer said.

Doug shook his head. "Why would anyone...?"

"Can you think of anyone that might want some kind of revenge?" the corporal asked.

"Revenge? I can't imagine why," Dad said, aghast.

"Looks like someone doesn't want to see you succeed," Corporal Fraser said.

"But the whole community is supportive. It's bringing business to the area," explained Dad.

"Dr. Roost thinks it's sabotage too," Daniel piped up.

Corporal Fraser nodded. "Sure looks like it."

"But why?" asked Pederson, bewildered. "We haven't done anything to anyone."

"At least, not that we're aware of," added Mildred.

Pederson stared at her in shocked confusion, the way cattle do when they touch an electric fence that wasn't there before.

"But *who*?" He began coughing and Dr. Roost walked with him over to a shady spot under an overhang, where they sat on a ledge and watched the proceedings.

Once he'd examined the site, Corporal Fraser allowed Daniel and Mildred to take photographs with their cameras, telling them what he needed for official documentation, including the use of a tape measure to indicate the scale of what was being documented. Ole Pederson then instructed Craig and the men in preparing plaster of Paris samples of the tire tread marks and the almost obliterated footprints. While they waited for them to dry, Dad, Doug, Craig and Corporal Fraser fanned out and examined the tire tracks across the hills.

When Corporal Fraser indicated it was okay to go back to the site, Daniel squatted beside the mound of dirt the thieves had disturbed, gently searching through the dirt. Dr. Roost and Ole Pederson peered over his shoulder. Several handfuls later, he found a small bone fragment and handed it to Mr. Pederson.

"Hard to say what it is; could be part of a foot bone." The old man caressed it.

Daniel stared at the empty bed. Fragments too tiny to be of much use lay scattered about, but the main sections were long gone. They might find something more buried deeper, but there was no way of knowing that and additional bones wouldn't be of much value without the skull.

Daniel watched the trackers disappear over another rise. "Doesn't seem like we can do much more here. Maybe we should go back to the house."

"Might as well," agreed Dr. Roost.

"Hrmmph," Pederson grunted and began climbing the hill, still muttering to himself, his back hunched, his strides a little less sure.

Mildred Roost sighed. "I'm worried about Ole. You know what this means to him."

"Surely we'll find the *Stygimoloch!*"

"I wouldn't count on it, Daniel. Even if we find the remains, they may be badly damaged."

Daniel wondered how they were going to find the culprits. Surely it couldn't be anyone from the community. But then why would anyone *anywhere* want to sabotage the operation? He hoped Corporal Fraser would come up with some clues soon. Otherwise, where would they start looking?

As Daniel contemplated the disaster, he wondered why Todd hadn't rushed to the site with the others. He'd thought Todd wanted to come with them to the dig this morning, but then he'd said that he'd better finish the harvesting. That must be what he was doing. Surely Todd couldn't be involved – could he?

CHAPTER THREE

As Daniel walked back to the farmyard with Mr. Pederson and Dr. Roost following some distance behind, he thought about the missing fossils. They had lost not only months of research and painstaking work, but also the exciting proof that the species had existed in Saskatchewan. He would never forget the devastated look on Ole Pederson's face. As he shuffled across the yard, Dactyl came to greet him and licked his hand as if he knew how distraught Daniel felt.

When Daniel reached the house, his mom, Greta Lindstrom, Lucy and the two younger girls with Cheryl between them emerged from the outdoor kitchen and Jed arrived from the campsite.

"All that work gone!" Mom hugged Daniel tight.

"We can only hope the RCMP can pick up the trail." Greta shook her head in dismay.

Daniel pulled away and caught sight of Todd Nelwin

walking slowly towards them. The stony look on his face puzzled Daniel.

"Did you hear the news?" Daniel asked.

Todd nodded. Daniel wondered if something was bothering him.

"Can we go help search?" Lucy asked.

"Yeah, let's go look," her two younger sisters said.

Daniel's mom raised her hand. "Corporal Fraser is there, so we'll wait and see what he has to say." She and Greta herded everyone toward the outdoor kitchen.

Lunch was a sombre affair. Even Jed's sisters were quieter than usual, taking Cheryl outside as soon as they'd finished eating. Everyone looked up when Dad came in with Craig, Doug and Corporal Fraser. Todd sat quietly, staring down at his plate.

Dad shook his head. "No sign of where the tracks lead."

"We picked up a bit of a trail about a mile east," said Corporal Fraser, "but it petered out and there's no way of knowing which way the thieves headed after that."

"There are several sets of tire tracks out there," said Doug. "And lots of footprints."

"We brought the casts back with us so we can compare them. We'll have to eliminate all of you first, of course," Corporal Fraser said.

"We can do that right after we finish lunch," Mom suggested.

Amid the babble of other suggestions from everyone in the kitchen, Daniel noticed that Todd still said little.

Whenever Daniel looked at him, he saw a flash of uneasiness in Todd's eyes. The little hairs on Daniel's arms tingled. He decided to keep a close watch on Todd.

When the comparisons were done between everybody's shoes and plaster casts from the scene of the theft, Corporal Fraser concluded that there were at least two and maybe three thieves. "It's almost impossible to tell, because you have visitors here everyday. The only way we could prove anything would be in a backwards kind of way."

Daniel attempted to figure out what that meant.

"I can see you're puzzled, Daniel," smiled Corporal Fraser. "What I mean is, if the footprints turn out to be from someone you know for sure has never been here as a visitor, then we might have something to work with." He continued to explain, "Of course, that won't help us until we find the culprits and compare their shoe prints."

"I get it now," said Daniel. "If you have suspects and they deny being here, you can prove they were by their prints."

"Yes, but that's a very long shot and still doesn't prove they stole anything."

"But what about the tread marks from the vehicles?"

Corporal Fraser said, "I have to run them through the system, but I'm fairly certain they're from all-terrain vehicles. I don't know if we can isolate the exact ones until the treads are studied, but the casts will help."

"Just one ATV?" asked Ole Pederson.

"I'd say at least a couple of them, and maybe with trailers attached," suggested the officer.

"I guess we have our work cut out for us," Pederson said.

"No," interjected Corporal Fraser, "*you* don't. We do, meaning the police force. Let us deal with the situation." He surveyed them all. "That goes for every one of you."

They all nodded in agreement, though Daniel crossed his fingers loosely behind his back. He still wanted to see what he could find out.

"Could I suggest that we keep the type of dinosaur to ourselves?" asked Pederson. "We're trying to keep its discovery a secret until we have confirmed all the evidence. Only a couple of experts at the museum know anything about it. We don't want the media or the public to know yet."

"Sure thing," agreed Corporal Fraser. "Besides, it's always good to keep some information back to compare with evidence that comes in which might lead us to an arrest."

"The more discreet you can be about everything the better," Dr. Roost added.

"I can even try and keep back that it's a dinosaur skeleton we're looking for from your place, at least for a day or so while we do a general inquiry," offered Corporal Fraser. "But eventually it will have to come out if we need the public's help in locating it."

"Fair enough," said Pederson.

Corporal Fraser left shortly afterwards. Lucy and Jed continued to take the last of the visiting groups on tours of the quarry for the rest of the afternoon. Meanwhile, the adults tidied up the kitchen, yard and campsite, and mulled over what they should do about the sour turn of events. Daniel managed to slink away, rounding up his horse, Gypsy.

Not bothering with a saddle, Daniel flung himself onto his grey pinto mare, loping bareback across the fields. He avoided the tour groups, circling wide around the quarry. Approaching the area where the tracks led away from the site, he scanned the hard ground looking for impressions. In an ever-widening circle, he searched, but there was nothing visible.

As Daniel headed home, several flocks of honking geese flew south in wide Vs across the bright blue sky. He guided Gypsy to the edge of the drying pasture and they entered the ditch along the grid road. As they crossed a dirt trail into a field that neighboured the Bringham land, Daniel pulled Gypsy to a sudden halt.

A forty-five gallon metal barrel with a gash in it lay on its side, spilling oil into the ditch that drained into a nearby stream. Had it fallen off a load by accident, or had someone dumped it there on purpose? Either way, Daniel had to do something fast before the contaminated stream reached the main creek that flowed across their land.

Although the oil spill was relatively small compared to oil tanker leaks on the oceans, Daniel knew the negative ecological effects could last for many years. Besides the damage that would be caused to the land, birds and animals could die from drinking the water or eating contaminated plants. Daniel wheeled Gypsy away from the dangerous area and raced home.

Back in the yard, Daniel found Mom and Greta drinking coffee at the picnic table with recipe books spread out in front of them. When he explained what he'd found, Mom raced to the house to call Dad on his cell phone and then to advise the local environmentalist group.

Within minutes, Dad and Doug arrived from the campsite. Daniel helped them gather ropes, a tire jack, pails, rags and other equipment, including rubber gloves and face masks for themselves. They placed everything on the stoneboat, while Doug hitched his Jeep up to it. Daniel was just about to hop in, when Dad stopped him.

"You stay here, Daniel," he advised. "It could be dangerous if there are any toxic fumes and I don't have another mask for you."

Disappointed, Daniel stepped back and watched the men drive out of the yard. Already a stream of vehicles was heading past their farm on the way to the danger zone. He knew it would take several hours to ensure the habitat was thoroughly cleaned and he might as well do something else. He still had Gypsy to see to. He'd left her tied by the water trough.

"Have you seen Mr. Pederson and Dr. Roost?" Daniel asked, as he walked Gypsy past Mom and Greta.

"They went to Eastend to talk to the paleontologists there," Mom said. "They're going to see what can be done to get the news discreetly out to various museums and contacts so they can keep watch for any unusual activity."

"What about Craig?" Daniel asked. "What's he doing?"

"He went to Eastend too. You weren't around or they would have asked you to go along."

Daniel nodded, feeling left out of everything.

"So is Todd still down at the campsite?" He nodded towards the valley below.

"Todd had to go home," Mom said.

"Why?" asked Daniel. Todd had never left early before. Did he know something?

Mom shrugged her shoulders. "He remembered something he had to take care of."

Daniel mounted his horse. "I'll go see if I can give him a hand."

"No, Daniel," Mom called out. "I don't want you going over there."

"I'll be fine." He nudged Gypsy forward.

"No! I don't want you anywhere near their dad or their dogs."

"Okay," Daniel reined Gypsy in reluctantly. "When will Mr. Pederson and the others be back?"

"Hard to say. They talked about stopping at other places along the way."

He guided Gypsy to the corral gate, slid off her back and opened the gate. Then he removed her bridle and released her.

As he headed to the house, Daniel wished he were with Mr. Pederson, Dr. Roost and Craig. There was nothing else for him to do except think of the problems they had. The oil spill would be cleaned up by the end of the day, but the loss of the *Stygimoloch* meant he and Pederson couldn't do any further research on the species, and there wasn't much information available about them.

The laboratory examinations of the fossils would have been so rewarding – especially as he'd seen a *Stygimoloch* in real life on his last trip to prehistoric time with Dr. Roost. They'd brought photographs back to help with their investigations, but that wouldn't mean much now. And they couldn't show the photographs to anyone, because no one would believe they weren't faked.

Daniel stopped in his tracks. There *was* one way of studying the *Stygimoloch*, but it was simply too dangerous. Besides, he'd promised himself he would give up travelling to the Cretaceous Period. He did have a way to go, though, because he had managed to bring back a pressed leaf and a small piece of branch – both keys to the doorway into the past. Daniel had hidden the specimens where he hoped no one would find them. He didn't want to chance anyone accidentally being transported into the time of the dinosaurs, as he had been before.

Wait a minute! Why was he even thinking about going back to the past? Did he *really* want to go? Daniel shuddered. No way! He continued walking to the house.

In the dining room, Daniel dug around in the bottom drawer of his dad's desk for the Rural Municipality map. Spreading it out on the table, he traced the various roads and trails, trying to guess where the load of fossils might have been hauled. But no one route stood out in his mind, even though he was more familiar with the local landscape than most people were, because he had travelled throughout the surrounding area many times while searching for dinosaur fossils. Was there something he hadn't considered? He closed his eyes and tried to imagine being a thief, but moments later Cheryl's nap waking-up chatter disturbed him. He hurried upstairs to retrieve her.

From her room, he waved out the window at Mom to let her know that he was taking care of his little sister. Putting her socks and shoes on, he led her downstairs and into the yard where Leanne and Lindsay snagged her and ran to the sandbox to play. Dactyl joined them with happy barks.

"Has Todd returned yet?" Daniel asked, sitting down at the picnic table beside Mom.

"No, but that's okay. None of us feel much like working today anyway."

Darn! Daniel would have to be patient until he could talk to Todd.

"Someone's in a hurry," commented Greta, motioning to the vehicle speeding down the gravel road in their general direction.

"Wonder where they're headed?" Daniel watched as waves of gravel dust swirled over the fields in the car's wake.

All of a sudden, the driver applied the brakes and skidded towards their approach.

"Who is that maniac?" Greta asked.

Within seconds, the 1989 Chevrolet Celebrity turned down their drive and screeched to a halt a few yards from where they sat.

"Adrian McDermott! From the newspaper office," Mom answered.

They all stared as the young man emerged and ran over to the passenger side, where he pulled out camera equipment, a tape recorder and a microphone. Flinging the straps on his shoulders, equipment dangling across his chest, Adrian McDermott looked like a pack mule. He hurried towards them in a clatter of banging gear.

"Good morning, ma'am. I'm here to interview you about your new developments." Daniel noticed the young man wasn't much taller than his mom. He was dressed in casual pants, a shirt and a blazer with patches on the elbows. His green eyes glowed with keen interest and he had a friendly smile on his face.

"I'm afraid you've had a wasted trip. There's nothing we can tell you since the last story you did," Mom said, with a pleasant smile.

"I heard something unusual was going on here with your dinosaur operation." He set his gear on the ground.

"I just want to be the first to break the news." He reached for his tape recorder and swung the microphone towards Mom.

"Mr. McDermott," Mom said firmly. "I'm sorry you came all the way out here on a wild goose chase, but..."

"Can you at least confirm that the RCMP came to your farm early this morning?"

Daniel felt his pulse racing. He was torn between wanting to give Adrian the story to get help in locating the missing fossils, yet hoping his mom would keep it secret. Mom's face was flushed and he could see her wrestling with how to be nice yet get him to leave without telling him what was going on. Daniel moved closer to her.

Mom shook her head. "We don't have anything that we can tell you at the moment."

"Something must have happened." He stared from one to the other. "I know they were here."

Greta shrugged, giving him a quick smile. "Well then, you already know the answer to your question."

The reporter picked up his camera bag. "I won't push it for now, but how about you promise me that when you're ready to talk that it'll be *my* exclusive story."

"If and when there is something of interest for the public to know, we'll be sure to let you know," said Mom, with an encouraging smile. "In the meantime, you might want to follow the story about the oil spill."

McDermott's face became animated. "When? Where?"

Daniel gave him quick directions, but before he'd even finished explaining, McDermott scrambled to his car and shoved all his equipment in beside him. Within moments, he gunned the car and whirled off.

"That certainly is a dedicated young man!" Greta said.

"I wonder how he got his information about the theft so quickly, though," Mom said.

Daniel chewed on his lip as he pondered the question. They'd been very careful to keep their knowledge about the *Stygimoloch* theft quiet. They'd only discovered it a few hours ago. Was someone close leaking information?

CHAPTER FOUR

While they discussed Adrian McDermott's sudden appearance, Ole Pederson and the others returned from town. Daniel rushed over to them even before Mr. Pederson could park his old Studebaker truck.

"Did you talk to anyone in town about the theft?" Daniel asked.

"And hello to you too," Ole Pederson said with a brief smile, as he exited the truck.

"Sorry," Daniel said. "But we just had Adrian McDermott here asking us questions."

"Did he actually ask about the theft?" Dr. Roost asked, coming around the front of the truck with Craig right behind her.

"No, but he sure knew something was going on out here."

"Well, we certainly didn't say anything," said Old Pederson. "He's probably just fishing to see what he can get out of us."

"You didn't tell him, did you?" asked Mildred Roost.

Daniel shook his head. "I'd like to know how he got wind of it." He turned to look at Craig.

"Don't look at me. I haven't talked to anyone," Craig said.

"If it will make you feel any better," said Dr. Roost, "we only went to the T. rex Discovery Centre and spoke to the general manager there, and then we talked to Tim Tokaryk and Wes Long in the lab. In Climax, we talked to the staff at the museum and the same at the one in Shaunavon, but we asked them all to keep everything confidential and I know they will."

"We did stop in to see how Corporal Fraser was doing, but we were only there briefly and no one else was about," added Ole Pederson.

Dr. Roost said, "Most likely one of the neighbours saw the RCMP car in the yard."

Pederson looked around. "I suppose Ed, Doug and Todd are still down working at the campsite? "

"Todd went home," Daniel said.

"He left?" interrupted Ole Pederson.

"He told Mom he needed to take care of something," Daniel said.

The focus turned to Craig. "Don't look at me. I don't have a clue why he left!"

"I'm sure he must have had a good reason." Mr. Pederson tried to brush the absence off, but Daniel noted the concern that clouded his grey eyes.

"So did Corporal Fraser have any news?" Daniel asked, pushing aside his own anxiety about Todd.

Pederson's body seemed to droop. "Nothing...and I'm not holding out any great hope..." A tickle seemed to catch in his throat as he talked, causing him to cough and his eyes to water.

"There's something else," said Daniel. He told them about the oil spill.

"Landsakes!" Dr. Roost protested. "What more can happen?"

Mr. Pederson looked even gloomier. "I think I'll just go home now," he said, reaching for a handkerchief from his pocket and wiping his eyes. "I'll talk to you all tomorrow. Keep me posted if there's any news about the fossils."

"We will," Daniel and Dr. Roost said together, as they watched Pederson shuffle back to his truck, looking like a much older man than he'd looked first thing that morning.

"If we don't get that *Stygimoloch* back, I worry what it will do to him," muttered Mildred Roost.

"Me too," Daniel whispered.

"He's more upset than I've ever seen him. Discovering the *Stygimoloch* specimen meant everything to him."

"We just *have* to get the fossils back!"

Dr. Roost seemed lost in her own world. "Wish I knew how we could do that. I'd give anything to see him inspired again." She wandered off, leaning on her cane as if she too had suddenly aged.

Daniel stood in the middle of the yard for some time, thinking of the look on Pederson's face. When he heard Mom and Cheryl returning from the henhouse, he headed off to begin evening chores. Craig was already in the barn, heaving bales.

By the time Daniel had finished milking, Todd had still not returned, so he and Craig completed the barn chores together. When they were almost done, Daniel asked him about his brother.

"I don't understand why Todd left," Craig admitted. "I'd better get home and see what's going on."

"Let us know if you need anything," Daniel said, as Craig hung the pitchfork on its usual nail on the wall stud and left.

Daniel leaned against a post and sighed. He was glad the day was almost over.

Lying in bed that night, he found himself haunted by the day's happenings and Mr. Pederson's look of despair. If only he could do something to bring back the old man's spirit.

Would taking Pederson on a journey into prehistoric time help him recover from this loss?

If he and Ole Pederson went, then Dr. Roost probably would insist on going too. She was brave, he had to give her that, but she wasn't spry enough to climb trees, nor was Mr. Pederson. What could they do instead to keep safe?

He thought of a series of pulleys and ropes, maybe with some kind of harness system to hold them on their way upwards. But that sounded too cumbersome if they needed to escape quickly. Or could they take some kind of stun gun or tranquilizer darts like the ones used on elephants and other large wild animals? But even if they could get their hands on such things, he was sure the dinosaurs had thicker hides, and even if the darts could penetrate them, there might not be much effect.

He'd do some research on the Internet when he had a chance. Maybe there was something that originally had a different purpose that they could use. He remembered reading a science fiction novel called *The Dechronization of Sam Magruder* in which a man had gone to the Cretaceous Period and existed there for years, having discovered that large dinosaurs like the *Tyrannosaurus Rex* had poor eyesight, and that if he stood close to them, they couldn't see him. But the book was a story and he seemed to recall that recent research indicated the *T. rex* actually had great eyesight. Daniel would wait and see what happened tomorrow. No point in rushing things.

But the next day was no different. Although the police were making inquiries and searching abandoned buildings, nothing had turned up. Every time a phone rang or someone drove into the yard, Daniel's stomach did a little flip-flop, but it was always quarry tour business.

There seemed to be an extra flurry of visitors trying to see the excavation before the season closed. The only thing that distracted Daniel from his worries was taking the odd group to the paleontological site. But this depressed him even more each time he arrived and saw the path that led to the devastation. Although he avoided taking any of the visitors to the *Stygimoloch* area, his thoughts were there and he could feel his enthusiasm drain away.

"This is really tough going," said Jed, as they took a break in the yard before the next groups arrived.

"Good thing today is the last day," Daniel agreed.

"Yes," said Lucy, joining them. "This should be a really happy day to celebrate the end of the summer and our success. Instead, everyone is moping around."

"I haven't even seen Dr. Roost yet today," said Lucy. "Your mom said she drove off without breakfast this morning."

Daniel nodded. "And Craig and Todd haven't put in an appearance all day either. And they didn't let us know they weren't coming."

"That is unusual. What do you think is up with them?" asked Jed.

Daniel shook his head. "Everything seems so strange now. Even Mr. Pederson didn't show up."

"But this is the last day," said Jed.

"I know," Daniel said. "But Dad stopped by to see him and he said he wasn't feeling well today, so he wasn't coming over."

"I don't like the sound of that," said Jed.

"Me either," Lucy agreed.

"Good thing we could manage taking his place as the guide at the quarry," said Jed.

"Maybe we should pay him a visit," Lucy suggested. By the time they had shown the last of the visitors off the property, though, it was late and Jed's parents wanted to head for home right away.

"We'll come by in the morning and take stock of everything," Doug Lindstrom said.

"Why not make it in a couple of days instead," Mom put forward. "Give yourselves a break."

Dad added, "Libby's right. We'll get to it over the next few days."

Daniel silently agreed. Even if Dr. Roost or Mr. Pederson came for breakfast, it would still be a nice change not to have an extra family around all the time as they'd done every day of the summer. Besides, now that the theft had happened, the planned prospecting tour for the next morning was called off.

Doug leaned out of his truck window. "Thanks, Ed. We could use a bit of time to get back on track at home before school starts."

Doug and Ed shook hands, and the Lindstroms pulled out of the driveway, with everyone waving from the crew-cab truck and Dactyl barking at the shouts from the youngest children.

"I'm going to head over to see how Mr. Pederson's doing," said Daniel.

"Don't be long," said Dad. "We still have evening chores to do and it looks like it's you and me tonight, son."

"Ask if there's anything we can do for Mr. Pederson," Mom suggested.

"I will. See you soon." Daniel whistled for Dactyl, who trotted up in moments. His dog was the only one that had any bounce left in him.

"Come on, boy!" Daniel gave his pet a scratch behind the ears and they set off.

All was silent as Daniel approached Mr. Pederson's shack. Should he disturb him? But then he remembered how two winters earlier Mr. Pederson had been quite ill. He probably wasn't anywhere near that sick right now, but still it would be good to see how he was doing.

Crunched into the side of the hill with a lean-to attached and desperately needing some paint, Pederson's place wasn't much to look at, Daniel thought, but its rough look also kept intruders out. As they neared the door, Dactyl noticed some movement in the brush close to the shack and wandered off to investigate.

Daniel knocked on the solid, rough-hewn door, quietly at first, and listened for a response. Then he banged louder and thought he heard a weak, "Come in."

The door creaked as he entered and stared into the gloom. Mr. Pederson lay on his cot in one corner of the room, but made no move to rise. Daniel walked over to his side. His friend seemed frailer than ever, his face sunken in.

"You okay, Mr. Pederson?" he asked.

"Just extremely tired," admitted the older man.

"Have you eaten today? Would you like me to make you something?" Daniel asked.

"Some tea and some cheese and biscuits would be nice." Mr. Pederson pointed to a cooler on the floor. "You'll find the food in there. Tea's in the thermos on the table. I brought it from town. I haven't bothered turning on a generator for power."

As Daniel bustled about preparing the snack, Pederson shuffled over to the table, but neither spoke of matters on their minds. Pederson's hands trembled as he accepted the cup of tea and nibbled on the crackers and cheese. His coughing seemed to have subsided, though, and Daniel thought that was a good sign, but the old man didn't seem to want to talk.

"Mom wants to know if you need anything."

"Only the *Stygimoloch* back." He grimaced and set his cup of tea down.

Neither one of them mentioned that even if the *Stygimoloch* fossils did turn up, there was no telling what condition they'd be in, but they were both thinking it. Daniel hated to see his old friend so miserable. Something had to be done to perk Mr. Pederson up.

Without thinking it through, Daniel blurted out. "How would you like to see the real thing?"

An instant sparkle lit up Mr. Pederson's eyes.

"You know I would." He tilted his head and looked at Daniel. "So you still have what you need to go back to the past?" he asked.

Daniel nodded.

"Grand!" Mr. Pederson sat up a little straighter. "Let's talk about how I can go."

"How *we* can go," corrected Daniel. "You and me."

Mr. Pederson shook his head. "No, I won't let you go."

"You can't go without me," Daniel protested. "You don't know anything about it or what to expect!"

"But I do!" said Mildred Roost's voice from the doorway.

Daniel groaned. He hadn't meant to talk about going back to the world of the dinosaurs, not yet. But the words were out, and there was no taking them back.

CHAPTER FIVE

"You didn't think you'd get away without me, did you?" Dr. Roost chortled.

Daniel hadn't heard her arrive. She must have parked the truck some distance away and walked from there to Pederson's. She thumped her cane across the old boards laid over packed dirt that served as the floor and settled herself in a chair.

"And I agree, young man, you are staying home. Ole and I can go by ourselves."

Daniel shuddered. "I don't think that's a good idea."

"I know all your reasons why and I agree. It is dangerous for us. We're not spring chickens any more. But I think with a few calculations we could come and go fairly quickly right close to where we saw the *Stygimoloch*." She grinned at Mr. Pederson.

"We'd just stay long enough to observe their feeding rituals and take a few pictures. We wouldn't venture anywhere else." She turned back to Daniel. "We'd be back before you knew it."

"How could you calculate where to go?" Daniel asked. He still didn't agree, but he was willing to hear what she had to say. Now he knew how his parents must feel when he tried to talk them into letting him do stuff they thought was dangerous.

"You already know the approximate place you land in the past whenever you leave from your hideout. And we know where we returned this last time was only a couple of hills away from where we are right now. We just need to draw up a map and measure some distances here, then see if we can't figure out how to land in the general location of the place where you and I saw the *Stygimoloch*."

"I see what you're saying, but some of that landscape was pretty tricky and we backtracked a couple of times," Daniel answered.

"I'm sure if we put our heads together and studied our photographs, we'd be able to pinpoint the spot fairly accurately." Dr. Roost's enthusiasm for a return trip was evident.

"What do you think?" Daniel asked Mr. Pederson.

"I think we need to consider this carefully, before we make a decision as to whether or not we go." Thank goodness. Mr. Pederson hadn't made up his mind yet.

"What's to think about?" asked Dr. Roost.

"The danger we'd be in, for one thing," replied Pederson. "I'd like to consider all the possibilities first."

Dr. Roost gave a brief rundown of what Ole Pederson could expect. As she spoke, Daniel could see the excitement grow in the old man's eyes.

"This seems too good of an opportunity to miss," he admitted. Maybe Pederson had made up his mind, after all.

"Indeed," said Dr. Roost. "We'll only be there for a short time."

"Very short," said Daniel, though he still worried about the old couple's stamina and about how they would cope for even a few minutes.

Pederson handed the teacup and the plate with crackers and cheese back to Daniel. "Here, get rid of that and grab some paper. There's some right over in that drawer." He indicated a dilapidated cabinet along one wall.

He turned to Dr. Roost. "We need to think it through carefully so you and I can make the most of it while we're there."

"Whoa, wait a minute," protested Daniel. "I still want to come with you."

"Too dangerous," Mr. Pederson and Dr. Roost said in unison.

"If you're only going for a few minutes, it'll be safe enough for me!"

"We'll decide that later," said Mr. Pederson, sidestepping the issue.

"Nope, I won't help you unless you let me come." He crossed his arms over his chest and stared at the pair.

Mr. Pederson grinned sheepishly at Dr. Roost. "I think he's got us."

"Yes, we need him to pull it off."

Daniel grinned at them. They sounded like they were planning a bank robbery. "Yep, without me you're not going anywhere."

"Fine, young man," said Dr. Roost. "Grab that paper and let's get started."

"It's a deal then? I come with you?"

Mr. Pederson gave a wry smile. "You drive a hard bargain."

"It's only fair," replied Daniel.

Daniel scurried over to the old cabinet to get the paper and a pencil.

"You'll need a ruler too," said Mr. Pederson. "You'll find one in the drawer with my cooking utensils."

Daniel lifted his eyebrows in surprise.

"I always know where it is if I keep it in there." The old man shrugged his shoulders.

Daniel found it and joined the other two at the table. Pederson began drawing the outlines of the surrounding land with the use of a ruler, plotting his shack and Daniel's hideout on the diagram.

"How do you know where they go?" asked Daniel.

"I know how many steps I take to get to places and how long my strides are," he answered, his eyes alight with interest. "It helps to keep track of where I've searched and where I've notated something unusual."

"This is a good start," Daniel said. "But for the Cretaceous Period, I'll need my notebook and the pictures, which are at home."

Dr. Roost nodded. "Yes, there's plenty of time to do that tomorrow. I'll see what I can remember and try to draw something to scale tonight."

"I'd better get back. I promised I wouldn't be long." Daniel turned to Mr. Pederson. "So will we see you at breakfast tomorrow?"

"Wouldn't miss your mom's cooking for anything!" he smiled.

"I'll give you a ride back, young man," said Mildred Roost.

"Thanks. My folks will be glad to see you've returned too. Everyone kind of disappeared today." He explained about the missing Nelwin brothers.

"Maybe they're having problems with their dad. They know they can come to us if they need to. But it's best to let them sort things out on their own until they ask for help," said Pederson, rising to his feet. "Come on, I'll walk you to the truck."

Daniel smiled to himself as he watched Mr. Pederson accompany Mildred Roost across the pasture to her parked truck. What a change his old friend had gone through since they'd begun talking about going back into prehistoric time. His step was lighter and his voice stronger. Even Dr. Roost was chattier than usual as they walked along, almost touching.

"Thank you for making an old man feel better, lad." Ole Pederson squeezed Daniel's shoulder. "I'm looking forward to finishing our plans tomorrow."

"I am too," said Dr. Roost. "We'll see you bright and early at the Bringhams' for breakfast."

"Bye, Mildred," Pederson said with a smile that lit up his eyes.

Dactyl appeared and hopped into the truck ahead of Daniel. On the ride home, Daniel sat lost in his thoughts.

"And what's that smirk doing on your face, young man?" asked Mildred Roost.

"Nothing," he answered.

"Whatever you're thinking probably isn't right," she retorted.

"Oh, I don't know," said Daniel. "I think Mr. Pederson's kind of sweet on you."

"Oh, bosh," she said. "We've known each other for years. We get along fine, that's all."

"You mean to tell me you're not sweet on him either?"

Dr. Roost squirmed a little and stepped on the gas without answering. After a moment, she said, "I think you're getting a mite too personal."

"I think I'm just getting too close to the truth," quipped Daniel.

"Maybe you are at that," she said quietly, as if to herself.

As they drove along, a companionable silence filled the cab of the truck. Daniel remembered how Mr.

Pederson's interest had been sparked and his attention diverted from the theft of his precious fossils. The only problem was that they'd actually have to travel back in time. He gave an involuntary shiver at the thought of the danger they'd be in. The only consoling thought was that they'd only be gone a short time – just long enough for Ole Pederson to see the *Stygimolochs* and to take a few pictures.

As if reading his mind, Mildred Roost said, "We'll plan this trip really well to minimize the risks. I'm sure we can estimate where we need to be within a very short distance."

"That will work if the *Stygimolochs* are still in the same grazing area," said Daniel, a little bit doubtful.

"True, but we can probably assume they're creatures of habit. We'll make sure we come right back either way," she reassured him.

"We'll need to stay close together at all times."

"Indeed. You and I can stay on either side of Ole. We'll keep a close watch on each other and grab him if we need to leave in a hurry."

"Sounds good," said Daniel.

He felt his stomach churning at the thought of entering the treacherous world of the dinosaurs again. The last time he'd gone, he'd barely made it out alive. What would it be like having two elderly people to keep an eye on? Having Dr. Roost with him had been bad enough, especially when they'd had to climb a tree.

Although Mr. Pederson was looking much better, he was still fairly frail, simply because of his age. But then, Mildred Roost had surprised him with her agility when they'd time travelled together; maybe things would be okay. Besides, they were only going for a few minutes.

When they returned to the yard, Mildred only stopped long enough to let Daniel out, honked hello to the Bringhams and continued to her parking spot on the far side of the yard. Daniel hurried to the barn. Dad had already milked the cows and Mom was doing the separating.

"Sorry, I'm late," said Daniel, grabbing a pitchfork and heading for the stalls. "I didn't mean for you or Mom to have to do the work."

"It's all right, Daniel," Dad said. "I think it was more important for you to spend time with Ole."

Mom came out of the separating room and poured some milk into the cats' bowl. Cheryl toddled behind her.

"This is kind of like old times, all of us out here doing the chores together, isn't it?" she said.

Daniel had to admit it was nice to share the work with his family. A warm feeling had replaced his sense of foreboding and for a little while as they worked, he forgot about their other problems.

"How is Mr. Pederson doing?" asked Dad.

"He'll be fine. He promised he'd be here for breakfast in the morning. He said he wouldn't miss Mom's cooking for anything."

Mom laughed. "Sounds like he's got some of his old spunk back."

"Dr. Roost will be here too," said Daniel. "She was at Mr. Pederson's."

"Guess I'll have to make something special then," said Mom, wrinkling her brow.

"How about Belgian waffles?" Daniel suggested.

"I think that could be arranged." She swung Cheryl onto her hip and left the barn. "I'll let you feed the separated milk to the calves and I'll get supper on. I've got the cream I need to whip for the morning."

"Sure thing," said Daniel, grabbing a bale and spreading the straw into the stall his dad had just cleaned.

When there was only one more stall to go, Daniel said, "I'll finish up here, Dad."

"Okay, son. I'll take you up on that. I want to get working on the books."

After a quick supper, Daniel wandered outside to spend some time with Gypsy. As he brushed her down, he thought again about Todd's sudden disappearance. Did this point to his guilt or to knowledge about the theft? And what was up with Craig not returning either? A thought popped into his mind. He'd been so busy thinking suspicious things about Todd that he hadn't considered whether there might be something wrong at their house. Maybe someone should go over and see if things were all right. They didn't have a phone, so they couldn't simply call.

Daniel returned the grooming tools to the barn and hurried to the house.

"Dad?" he called.

"In the dining room, son," Dad answered.

Daniel rushed in. "Do you think we should go over to the Nelwins and see if they're okay?"

Dad thought about it for a moment. "Maybe we should, but I hate to interfere in someone else's business, when we're not asked. There isn't really any good reason to go over."

"How about a purely social call? We could take some fresh cookies I baked this morning," Mom suggested from the doorway, where she held a squirming Cheryl wrapped in a fluffy blue towel after her nightly bath. "You and I could go and chat with Horace...tell him how well his sons are doing, that kind of thing."

Dad shrugged. "Sure, if you want to."

"Yes, I do. I agree with Daniel and something tells me we should check it out." She handed Cheryl over to Daniel. "How about you finish drying her off and get her into bed?"

Daniel sighed. He wanted to go with his parents, but he knew there was no point in arguing.

"Book," said Cheryl.

Daniel smiled. "Yes, I'll read to you. Come on." He carried her upstairs.

From the window in Cheryl's room, he watched his parents get into their car. Mom had her nursing bag in her hand. She often carried it with her, but Daniel was surprised she'd take it when they were only going a mile and a half away. Maybe she thought something had happened as well. Or maybe she was just being prepared.

By the time Daniel finished reading Cheryl her book three times and she'd settled down to sleep, he heard Mom and Dad returning. Quietly, he left his sister's room and slid down the banister in time to meet them at the kitchen door.

"Well?"

"There wasn't anyone home," said Mom, seeming even more puzzled than before.

"We drove around the yard, but there weren't any lights on anywhere," said Dad.

Mom said, "I wouldn't let your father get out of the car with all those vicious dogs."

"The family was probably out somewhere," suggested Dad. "We have no business nosing into their affairs."

"You're right, Ed," Mom said, "but still I wonder if they're okay."

"Hard to say," said Dad, heading back to the dining room. "Well, I have to get back to my paperwork. The bank is expecting a financial report by Tuesday."

"Thanks for going anyway, Dad, Mom," Daniel said, although he was disappointed with the outcome.

Getting ready for bed, his thoughts turned to the things they'd need for the journey to dinosaur time. They were only going for five minutes, tops, but he wanted to be able to take advantage of every opportunity. Dr. Roost would have her digital camera, but he'd take his as a backup.

He fell asleep still making plans.

CHAPTER SIX

After chores and breakfast the next morning, Daniel headed back to his room, where he grabbed his prehistoric photographs of *Stygimoloch* and some reference books. Next he went to his secret hiding place under the shelf in the bottom of his closet. He removed the elastic-bound notebook he'd used during his last visit to the past and turned to the page where the prehistoric leaf lay preserved. He breathed slowly and avoided direct contact with it — one slip and he'd be flung totally unprepared into the perilous world of the dinosaurs. Then he gently turned to the last page, where he found the tiny branch he'd carved off an ancient tree in the past still inside its plastic bag. Securing the elastic bands around the notebook once again, he slipped it into a large Ziploc bag and tucked it into his backpack.

By the time he gathered his research and made it downstairs, he found Ole Pederson's truck running outside the back door with Pederson and Dr. Roost already seated inside. Daniel smiled to himself at how eager they were to work on the project.

"I'd better double-check with Mom that it's all right if I take off for a while," Daniel said to Pederson through his rolled-down window.

"Already taken care of," Dr. Roost said from the passenger side. "I told her we had important things to be done. And make no mistake, we do."

Later, seated around Pederson's table, Dr. Roost spread out the map she'd drawn the night before. Daniel was surprised to see how detailed it was. As he made tea for them all from the thermos of hot water Mr. Pederson had brought from Daniel's mom, the old couple worked away on the maps and examined the photographs with a magnifying glass. Daniel added his calculations from the jottings and diagrams he'd made in his notebook.

"These documents are quite important to the study of geographical changes throughout the ages," said Pederson, using a pencil to add specific features that would help them align the two.

Dr. Roost nodded. "One of our maps represents the Cretaceous Period and the other represents our present time. In between these periods came the ice ages, the beginnings of the first human societies and all the rest of human history."

Daniel thought about the implications. "It's incredible even to think about the spot right here where we're sitting and how it used to be." He pointed to the spots on the two maps.

"It's amazing, all right." Ole Pederson sat back in a contemplative mood. "And going back to that time is the most profound thing I could do in my life. I could never have dreamed I'd be planning to see actual Cretaceous Period creatures. I'm still concerned about the dangers, but I can hardly wait to go." He rubbed his hands gleefully.

All at once, he went still. "Why don't we go right now?"

"Whew!" Dr. Roost chortled. "We're hardly prepared."

Daniel looked up from the maps. "Are you serious?"

"Why don't we just pop in for a couple of minutes and let me get the feel of it? Then I'll have a better idea of what I need to take," Mr. Pederson said.

"That would be crazy," spluttered Mildred Roost. "What's gotten into you, anyway? It's one thing to get going on the planning, but quite another to go too hastily."

"I just want a quick glimpse, that's all," grumbled Pederson.

"But it's so unlike you not to want to be totally prepared," Dr. Roost said.

"I've been prepared all my life," said Pederson, "and where has it got me? The greatest discovery I've ever made was stolen from me and I'm right back at square one. Except now I have a chance to do something truly spectacular and I want to experience it as soon as I can."

"Well, you don't want to put yourself or us in danger while you're satisfying some whim, you silly old fool," Dr. Roost scolded.

Daniel eyed her carefully. The idea wasn't that crazy, but maybe she was scared to go. Even more than he was.

"All I'm suggesting is a quick look," Pederson said.

"But I don't have my good hiking boots on or my backpack with all my stuff," she objected.

Mr. Pederson guffawed. "Well, then how about Daniel and I just drop in for a minute? I want to see how this all works."

When he felt Ole Pederson's eyes on him, Daniel felt his pulse increase along with his breathing. "I g-g-guess we could go right away," he spluttered out.

"All right, do you have that leaf we need or not?" Pederson demanded.

"How did you know that's what I had?" asked Daniel.

"I didn't for sure, but you've just confirmed it," smiled Pederson. "I knew it had to be something flat to fit in your notebook. So did you bring it?"

Daniel gulped. "Yeah, I did, but I didn't really expect to be going today."

"Don't tell me I have *two* chicken-hearted partners," he said.

"You won't be calling us that when you've seen what we have!" Dr. Roost said indignantly.

"So show me," Pederson goaded them.

"We're not falling for that trick, Mr. Pederson," said Daniel. "I've used that one on Cheryl to get her to do something I want her to do, so give me some credit."

Pederson laughed sheepishly. "Okay then, why don't you explain to me again how the time travel thing works."

"First off, we all have to stick together," Daniel said. "I mean that very seriously."

Pederson nodded.

"We have to be in contact so that we can all travel through time at once," Daniel continued. "When I touch the leaf, you'll be connected to me and we'll instantly go. If I drop it or we lose it and we're not touching each other, you'll be stuck there and there's no coming back for whoever is left behind."

"Do you have to hold the leaf the whole time we're away?" asked Pederson.

"No, I usually put it in my pocket. But as soon as I drop it – when it's no longer touching me – I come back with whoever is connected to me."

"Okay, I've got that all straight. I have no intention of straying from either of you," said Pederson. "So shall we give it a whirl?"

"We haven't even discussed where we'll leave from," Dr. Roost protested.

"Details. Let's just pick a spot and go for a few moments."

"We can't do that, Mr. Pederson," Daniel said. "We don't want to end up in the middle of the sea!"

"That's for sure," agreed Dr. Roost. "It's slimy and the bottom sucks at your feet like quicksand, not to mention the hungry creatures lurking about."

Daniel added, "We have to be prepared in case we have to hide somewhere right away."

"You sure don't want to be standing right in front of a *T. rex* with his mouth hanging open." Dr. Roost looked at Pederson crossly.

Meekly, Mr. Pederson sat back. "Yes, you're right. I've waited this long. Guess I can wait a few more hours."

"Hours?" Dr. Roost stood up. "We can't go today!"

"Why not?" Pederson looked at her in surprise. "We can gather everything we need over the next couple of hours, surely." He looked at Daniel. "How much time do you need?"

"I suppose I could be ready in an hour or so. Maybe we could go after lunch."

Pederson turned to Dr. Roost, "Mildred?"

"I suppose we could go then, but I still don't understand what the hurry is."

"And I don't see the need to wait," said Pederson.

Daniel had never seen the old man quite so determined. He seemed to have stopped worrying about the implications of what they were about to do.

"All right, then, you two are the experts. Where shall we leave from?" Pederson bent to study the maps.

"I'd say about halfway between here and my hideout," Daniel estimated.

"Near where you and Mildred returned this last time?" asked Pederson.

"No, a little closer to my hideout and a little bit more to the east — more towards the quarry." He pointed to a spot on the map.

Dr. Roost used the pencil to mark the spot. "I'd say that's about right, Daniel. We saw the *Stygimolochs* when we were nearly across that meadow, which I think is about here."

"All right, that's where we'll leave from after lunch," Pederson said confidently.

But at lunchtime Daniel could hardly eat a thing, even though Mom had prepared lemon meringue pie for dessert.

"Are you feeling okay?" Mom asked.

"I'm fine," he said. "Just a little disappointed that there's been no news from Corporal Fraser, I guess."

"That's enough to put us all off our feed," said Dr. Roost, swilling back the last of her tea.

"I'm not leaving any crumbs," said Pederson, wiping off the last of the meringue from his chin.

"I'm glad to see you're a little more chipper," said Mom. "What do you attribute that to?"

Pederson and Dr. Roost sat there with stony faces, not knowing what to say and not wanting to tell a lie. Daniel finally found his tongue.

"We're working out some strategies that might help find more information about the *Stygimoloch*. We've been studying maps of the area," Daniel answered truthfully.

"Yes, and we'd better get back to it," suggested Dr. Roost, kicking at Mr. Pederson under the table.

"Indeed! Thanks for another fabulous meal, Libby. I especially enjoyed the pie!" said Ole Pederson.

"You're quite welcome. There's enough left over for a coffee break this afternoon, if you're interested," she added with a pleased smile.

"I may just take you up on it," Mr. Pederson said. "A fellow can get awfully hungry when he's doing research." He began chatting about the merits of flavourful and enticing food.

"Come *on*, Ole," begged Dr. Roost.

Daniel laughed. Was Mr. Pederson having second thoughts about going to prehistoric time? Was he stalling by talking to Mom?

"All right, Mildred, I'm coming," he insisted. "Can't a fellow even give the cook a few compliments?"

"You're acting like this might be your last meal," snorted Mildred Roost.

Ole Pederson scoffed. "If it was, this is exactly what I'd like to have."

"Are you going too, Daniel?" Mom asked.

"Yes, if that's okay with you." Daniel never considered he might have to stay and do something. That would spoil all their plans. Although he wouldn't mind a little more time to prepare before they leaped into the past.

"Sure, just as long as you don't go far and you're back to do evening chores."

"No problem," he answered, not daring to look at either Dr. Roost or Mr. Pederson for fear of giving himself away.

Dr. Roost finally shepherded Pederson outside.

"What was that all about?" she demanded as they climbed into Pederson's truck. "You suddenly get cold feet or something?"

Ole Pederson looked abashed. "I guess subconsciously I had a few moments of concern, but I'm okay now. Let's go."

He put the truck into gear and they pulled out of the yard and across the pasture. Within minutes, they were at the spot they'd decided was the perfect place to depart from. They all got out of the truck and gathered their belongings without saying a word.

Dr. Roost strapped a whistle around her neck, along with her digital camera, then slung on a backpack and adjusted her Tilley hat. She also wore a waist pack with a small notebook and pencils. Ole Pederson carried the binoculars around his neck, put his sunglasses onto his head and pulled his hat down tight overtop. For people who'd prepared in a hurry, they had an impressive amount of gear between them. Daniel's own backpack, which he always had prepared for fossil searching expeditions, held extra water, matches, a regular camera, lots of pencils and, of course, his notebook, which contained the precious leaf and tiny branch.

When they were all assembled, Daniel took out his notebook and gently let the prehistoric leaf flutter onto a large rock. Keeping his eye on it, he returned his notebook and adjusted his backpack and clothing. Then he looked at his companions.

"Ready?" he asked, trembling slightly.

"Ready," they said in unison, stepping close to him. Their faces were stoic, but their eyes glowed with anticipation.

"Okay, hang on to me."

Daniel felt each of them grab onto an arm. Mr. Pederson raised an eyebrow and nodded. Dr. Roost, her lips tightly closed, squeezed Daniel's arm.

Without any further hesitation, he stooped down and picked up the leaf. In an instant, everything went black and a surge of energy went through them.

Daniel heard Pederson gasp beside him. Dr. Roost gave a little yelp on his other side. They were staring at an exquisite view of towering trees, huge draping leaves, moss-covered ground and lush ferns. The moist air hit them instantly, and Daniel quickly scanned their environment from the ground up and from side to side. Dr. Roost kept watch behind them. Mr. Pederson seemed stunned by the new world of colour, sights and sounds, and said nothing. Nor did he move.

He simply absorbed their surroundings, taking in the screeches of the huge birdlike creatures circling in the vibrant blue sky, high above the immenseness of the redwood and pine trees. As Dr. Roost took the opportunity to snap a few shots in every direction, Mr. Pederson began to study the vegetation at their feet.

He bent down for a closer look at vines and tiny flowers intermingled on the forest floor. He examined them gently and slowly, as if memorizing every detail, then wrote information in a little notebook that he drew from his pocket. Next he looked at cycads and large-leafed plants, then at the trees.

As Daniel continued to check for possible dangers, he held the leaf tightly in his hand. There was no need to tuck it away. They would be returning almost immediately.

A sudden rustling in the bushes alerted him, and he touched both of his companions to warn them. Mr. Pederson rose and they reached out and grabbed Daniel's arms once again, watching with pounding hearts for what was about to emerge.

Daniel grinned when he saw a rat-sized *Purgatorius* scuttle through the undergrowth. It squeaked with surprise when it ran over the unfamiliar terrain of Pederson's shoes.

"Whew!" Dr. Roost breathed a sigh of relief, but she kept checking in all directions.

Ole Pederson brought his binoculars to his eyes and scanned the horizon to his right. He pointed to a narrow path that led to a small, open meadow. Nodding his head, he motioned that he'd like to go in that direction. Without saying a word, Daniel and Dr. Roost considered the option and, peering about once more, silently nodded agreement.

The three moved as quietly as they could to the path. Clinging to one another, they progressed single file through the dense foliage. Dr. Roost led the way, with Daniel in the middle. Mr. Pederson followed, wide-eyed.

At the edge of the clearing, Dr. Roost stopped short and held her finger to her lips. They all listened intently. Something that made a *whoosh, whoosh* sound was coming their way. A dark shadow loomed overhead. They all ducked. Daniel pulled Dr. Roost and Mr. Pederson off the trail and tight against a huge tree trunk. As they stared upwards, a baby *Pteranadon* landed on a branch overhead.

"Are they dangerous?" Pederson whispered.

Daniel nodded and whispered back, "I was attacked by one."

Dr. Roost motioned behind them to the opening in the trees. Daniel turned and found himself staring at a small group of *Stegoceras* in a clearing, as they grazed on leaves, twigs and other low plants. Shorter than Daniel, they had domed heads with a fringe of horny knobs along the back of their thick skulls. Pederson seemed fascinated by the way they used their short forelimbs to grasp their food while they kept their balance using their large stiff tails and powerful rear legs.

All of a sudden, two meat-eating *Troodon*-like creatures bounded out of the trees. Mr. Pederson gasped and raised his binoculars. The lead *Stegoceras* sounded a bugle-like alarm and the herd raced away, trying to keep their young in the middle for safety. Dr. Roost captured a couple of photographs, nearly dropping her camera in the process.

"*Zapsalis*," she whispered.

Unfortunately, one young *Stegoceras* seemed to become confused and strayed slightly away from the others. The *Zapsalis* pursued it and isolated it from the herd. Within minutes, the juvenile *Stegoceras* was down and ripped apart.

"Just like a lion pursuing a herd of wildebeest!" Mr. Pederson seemed amazed. "Obviously an ancient hunting technique in the animal kingdom."

Dr. Roost continued to click away with her camera, though she made small gagging noises in the back of her throat. "Never did like violence," she admitted.

Suddenly, the *Zapsalis* abandoned their meal. The next thing Daniel knew, they were bounding across the clearing towards them. With the *Pteranadon* above them, and the *Zapsalis* almost on them, they were trapped.

"Time to leave!" Daniel yelled.

Dr. Roost and Mr. Pederson nodded frantically. The *Zapsalis* were only a few metres away, so close they could see their fierce eyes, gleaming with anticipation of their first delicious human meal.

"Everyone hang on!" Daniel felt the leaf clutched in his hand. He made sure Mildred Roost and Pederson were touching him.

Just as the *Zapsalis* sprang, he dropped the leaf.

CHAPTER SEVEN

Daniel saw a split second of darkness, heard a sharp whizzing sound and then he was once more looking at the rolling hills of the familiar pasture. Beside him, Pederson stood speechless. Mildred Roost shook herself and moved to Pederson's side.

"You okay, Ole?" She stroked his arm.

Pederson spoke like a person under some kind of magic spell. "I'll never forget this as long as I live!"

"I'm sure you won't," Dr. Roost said.

He blinked and seemed to see them more clearly. "We're going to have to give some serious thought about what to take when we go back."

"I don't know that I want to go back," declared Dr. Roost. "That might just have been enough for me. I'd forgotten how many dangerous creatures there were about."

Daniel agreed. "That was a little too close for comfort!"

"I think we were slightly off the mark in our calculations too," suggested Dr. Roost.

"Not by much. I think we should have launched about twenty metres to the east," Daniel said. "But it was just bad luck to run into the *Zapsalis*. They could have been anywhere."

Pederson was totally focused now. "We'll just have to make a few adjustments before we go again."

Daniel and Dr. Roost looked at one another with fear in their eyes. Daniel really wasn't keen on going back. And then he remembered something important.

"I don't have the leaf anymore," he admitted, not looking at either of them. He crossed his fingers behind his back. "We can't go back." He didn't want to tell them about the tiny branch, hoping the first trip had been enough of an adventure for Mr. Pederson.

He noticed Dr. Roost let out a breath of relief.

Ole Pederson stared at Daniel in disbelief. "How could we all have forgotten that important detail?"

Daniel shuffled uneasily, watching Pederson to see how he was taking the news. Although he had a look of dismay, he didn't seem extremely perturbed.

"That's what comes of rushing, I guess," said Dr. Roost. "I can't deny that I'm relieved."

"You really wouldn't go again if you had the chance?" Pederson asked.

"I'm not saying that exactly, but I'd make sure we had plans for being a little safer." Dr. Roost glared at Pederson. "I told you we needed more time to prepare!"

"How about you, Daniel?"

"This research is important, but maybe not worth it if we lose our lives," he admitted.

"So you have nothing else in your bag of tricks to take us back again?" Pederson asked.

Daniel tried to look innocent. Keeping his crossed fingers behind his back, he shook his head "no."

"Too bad." Pederson grimaced, but his eyes didn't show any distress. "So tell me, can anyone bring back something from the past to make it work?"

Daniel and Dr. Roost looked suspiciously at Pederson, but he kept his face absent of emotion, as if it was just something he was curious about.

"I suppose it would work for anyone," Daniel said reluctantly. He could feel butterflies flipping in his stomach. "Why?"

Pederson tilted his head, and with a little smile admitted, "I may just have a little something we could use."

"Ole, you don't." Dr. Roost seemed agitated about the prospect.

"Yes, I do. I picked up some vegetation along the way. I've got it in my backpack." Pederson slid the pack off his shoulder and patted it.

"Leave it there!" said Daniel, stepping away from him. "The moment you touch it, you'll be flung into the past."

"That's what I figured," said Pederson. "So Mildred, will you go with me again?"

She hesitated. "Only if we take time to really prepare for our safety," she admonished.

"I'm in, if you two are!" Daniel declared, not wanting to leave them on their own.

"No, you're not," Mr. Pederson and Dr. Roost said in unison.

"We're perfectly capable of going on our own!" Pederson said. "And I have the means to do it."

"But I know the terrain better than either of you," Daniel protested.

"Maybe, but we'll manage." With a mischievous grin, Pederson said, "We outwitted *you* this time, lad!"

"You definitely aren't going, and that's final." Dr. Roost waved a finger at Daniel.

Daniel groaned and shook his head at his two conniving companions. But he let them think they had outsmarted him, although he still had some ideas up his sleeve.

"Well, let me at least help you make your arrangements," he said.

"That would be appreciated and welcomed," Pederson said.

"How about we go back to the farm and see what's going on," Dr. Roost suggested. "I could use a break."

The other two agreed. Pederson dropped them back off in the yard. Daniel saw the rest of his family in the garden and planned to head that way. Then he noticed Dr. Roost lean back into Pederson's truck and heard her offer to drive him to an appointment with his doctor the next day. So there was something wrong with him after all.

Maybe Pederson shouldn't be going into the past. He should speak to Dr. Roost, but she had already gone into the back of her little camper truck and shut the door firmly. Pederson waved at Daniel and zoomed back out of the yard.

Daniel joined his family picking pumpkins and other squash in the garden. As he worked, he considered ways of making it safer to travel in prehistoric time. He tried to think of substances that would immobilize large dinosaurs. He'd recently read about an alligator in the United States being doped with the dental anaesthetic halothene so researchers could study its digestive system. Would something like that work? He had no idea where they could get it, or how much they would need.

Another problem would be applying it. Could they use a spraying system like those used for ridding an area of mosquitoes? What would the drift factor be like? Maybe they could wear some kind of oxygen masks.

This was getting more complicated by the minute. Even if they could get all the equipment, they certainly wouldn't want to be hauling heavy gear around. Daniel tucked the ideas into the back of his mind until he could check out some information on the Internet.

Once they finished harvesting the pumpkins and squash, they all turned to cleanup of the vines. When the family was almost done the garden work, the topic of the Nelwins came up.

"I sure hope nothing serious has happened to the boys," said Mom.

"Maybe we'll take another run over after supper." Dad turned to Daniel.

"Yes, I know," Daniel said before his dad could speak. "Take care of Cheryl."

Mom laughed. "I guess we do tell you that a lot."

Dr. Roost never emerged from her truck camper the rest of the afternoon, so Daniel didn't have a chance to speak with her about his theories or about Mr. Pederson. He did some research on his computer and came up with several other possibilities for halting attacks from various dinosaurs. If they couldn't get any halothene, maybe they could find some liquid nitrogen to cool the body and slow activity down. Maybe Dr. Roost had some pull somewhere to get some.

But he didn't know how much of either of these chemicals would be needed for such huge, agile creatures, or how quickly they would take effect. He didn't want to kill the creatures, just subdue them so they could study them a little in safety. He had a sudden thought. What about laser lights? Although they could cause blindness, maybe they would work as a temporary measure to slow down a dinosaur. He was still thinking this all through when he headed to the barn to do chores.

Dad noticed his distraction and set him to work milking the cows, while he fed the other livestock and chickens. Together they finished cleaning the stalls.

When Dad left to get a hammer from the tool shop to fix something in the kitchen, Daniel headed directly to the house with the milk pails. Mom wanted whole milk tonight for special bread dough, so he didn't need to do any separating.

After supper, Daniel offered to do the dishes so his parents could check on the Nelwins right away. He finished quickly as Cheryl chattered to him from her high chair, then swept his sister off for her bath.

While she splashed and got him wet, part of his mind was on what might be happening at the Nelwins. He wondered again if they were somehow connected with the *Stygimoloch* theft. There had been no word from Corporal Fraser all day, either, and they hadn't heard again from the reporter, Adrian McDermott.

By the time Daniel had tucked Cheryl into bed and read her a storybook, his parents had still not returned. They must have found someone home. This was probably good. At least they would find out what was going on. He lay down on the couch and watched television with the volume turned down low so he could hear when they returned. The next thing he knew, Dad was nudging him awake.

"Time to head for bed," Dad said, easing Daniel to his feet.

"How did it go?" Daniel asked, struggling to open his eyes.

"The boys were there, but Horace Nelwin is missing. They've been looking for him since last night. That's why they weren't home when we were there. They started searching for him again early this morning."

"They must be worried," said Daniel.

"He's never been gone this long before without them hearing from somebody about where he is." Dad rubbed his chin in thought. "We stopped to talk to a couple of the neighbours, but no one's seen him. Not even Corporal Fraser. We phoned him from the Milners."

"Wow!" said Daniel. His head was clear now. "What will happen next?"

"Nothing for now. If he doesn't turn up by morning, he'll be deemed a missing person and a bulletin will go out looking for him."

Daniel's eyes widened. "They'll put out an arrest warrant for him?"

Dad chuckled. "Well not quite that, but they will check hospitals and notify the network of police to check for him."

"Is his truck gone?" Daniel asked. "They could track him that way,"

"The funny thing is that it's not. But his ATV is missing," said Dad, scrunching up his face as he considered the possibilities.

"That doesn't sound good!" Daniel exclaimed. "He could be anywhere, maybe even lying injured out on the prairie somewhere."

"Yes, and a few neighbours have suggested we start looking for him in the countryside in the morning.

Corporal Fraser agrees. Of course, there's a chance he may just have gone some place to be alone. Or he could be sleeping off too many drinks somewhere," Dad said.

As Daniel mulled the information over, Dad guided him upstairs. "It's late, son. Try to get some sleep. We'll see if we can't get things straightened out in the morning."

"Will Craig and Todd be coming?"

"Yes, we've told them to make sure they come for breakfast and to bring us any news. They feel bad about not coming today, but we reassured them that we weren't angry."

"Yes," said Mom from the doorway. "The poor things didn't know whether to keep searching for their father or not, and then they were afraid to show up here late, so they just stayed away."

"I'm glad you went to check on them then," said Daniel, heading to the bathroom to brush his teeth.

"Yes, we had a nice long chat and told them they could come to us any time they had a problem," said Dad.

As he swished the toothbrush around in his mouth, Daniel wondered if Horace Nelwin's disappearance had anything to do with the fossil theft. Was it just a coincidence that both events occurred so close together? He still wanted to speak to Todd alone. He'd make sure to do that first thing in the morning.

His head whirled with images of the Nelwins, the absence of Horace and the missing *Stygimoloch* and the dinosaurs he'd soon be confronting again. He'd have to keep a close eye on Dr. Roost and Mr. Pederson too. He had no intention of letting them slip away without him. If they did manage it, he wouldn't be far behind them. As soon as he could the next day, he'd go over to Pederson's and help with the planning.

Partway through the night, he awoke from a nightmare. He'd been running from tree to tree, trying to escape the giant shadow of a *Pteranadon* that droned like an airplane overhead. He lay panting and it took him a long time to get back to sleep.

CHAPTER EIGHT

Daniel woke early the next morning and rushed to do his barn chores. He stopped short when he saw Todd heading towards him from the corral and Craig approaching from the barn, carrying pails of separated milk to the house.

"Morning," said Craig, setting the pail down with a sigh. "Everything's done."

"Whoa, you must have been up early," Daniel said.

"Didn't go to sleep," Todd answered, coming up to them. His clothes were all askew and crumpled and his bristly hair was flat in places. Craig's hair had an unwashed sheen to it and his wrinkled clothes had seen better days.

"Any word on your dad?" asked Daniel.

Both boys shook their heads.

Dad emerged from the tool shop and joined them. "Let's get some breakfast, then everyone can gather and search for him."

Dad herded them all towards the house. Once inside, he began the phone tree calls. In their district, they had set up a system where one person called two others, those two each called two more, and this procedure continued until everyone in the area was notified. Within minutes, Dad had arranged for all the neighbours to meet at the Nelwins in the next half hour. He called Corporal Fraser to confirm the arrangements. He'd just finished as Dr. Roost and Ole Pederson arrived for breakfast. Mom's waffles were an instant hit, but everyone gobbled them quickly and prepared to join the search party.

Daniel didn't have an opportunity to speak with Todd or Ole Pederson or Mildred Roost. Pederson winked at him across the breakfast table and Dr. Roost patted his arm, but otherwise the two kept to themselves. Even when he sidled up to them to see when they were meeting again, Dr. Roost motioned him to silence. He gave up and went to prepare for the search.

With Daniel on Gypsy, Todd and Craig saddled horses that had been used on the trail rides and they all headed out. At the Nelwins, they were joined by Dad on his ATV and Doug Lindstrom and Jed in their Jeep. The Nelwins' mean dogs had been locked in the barn to keep them from attacking anyone.

The rest of the neighbours soon arrived in various four-wheel-drive trucks, dirt bikes and other off-road vehicles. Corporal Fraser divided the surrounding area into quadrants, assigning several people to each one with instructions to call on their cell phones or return each hour to report on their progress.

Although the warm autumn sun beamed down on them, Daniel shivered. Thoughts of what he might find whirled in his mind like chips of ice in a blender. He, Craig and Todd swept out of the yard to search an area to the east, which covered several steeper gullies that were easier for their horses to navigate. As they rode away, they could hear the others calling for Horace.

For the first half a mile, the three of them walked their horses in silence a few yards apart. They examined small stands of trees and under bushes, keeping an eye out for tracks of any kind. Obvious deer and antelope trails criss-crossed on the hard ground, amid drying tufts of grass and the occasional clump of black-eyed Susans at the edge of the pasture. As they turned towards the centre of the quarter, the vegetation became scrubbier and more hilly. Tracks were harder to trace and there was no sign of human habitation anywhere.

After a while, they came to another fenced pasture that blocked their way, and decided it was time to head back and report in.

"Whose property is that?" Daniel asked before they turned around.

"Some people by the name of Collins homesteaded there, but there's nothing left anymore but a heap of rotting boards that was once their house," said Todd.

"Yeah, there's not even a road into the property anymore," Craig said, "I think Herb Milner bought it a few years ago. He rents it out for pasture land to Abe Johnson, I think. Or at least he did."

As they headed back to the Nelwins' place, they rode close to one another. At one point, Todd was nearly beside Daniel.

"Do you think your dad is out here somewhere?" Daniel asked.

Todd shook his head. "Nah, but if everyone thinks it will help to look for him, that's okay."

"Do you have any idea where else he might be?"

"Not really, but he might have just gone visiting or something."

Daniel stared at Todd. "You mean, he'd just up and go for a visit somewhere and not tell you?"

"It's possible," Todd answered, shrugging.

"But why? Has he ever done that before?" Daniel persisted.

But instead of answering, Todd made a point of guiding his horse around some rough terrain away from Daniel. Daniel had no choice but to skirt around in the other direction. Then Todd scooted ahead, so it wasn't convenient to question him anymore. His evasive manner told Daniel he either didn't want to talk or was hiding something.

Others had arrived back before them and no one had seen anything. They were just deciding whether or not to spread out farther and do another section, when another vehicle swirled into the driveway in a cloud of dust. Almost before the car had time to come to a full screeching stop, Adrian McDermott jumped out and scooped up his camera. He began snapping photographs of the searchers milling around, then sauntered closer to the group.

Corporal Fraser made his way through the throng.

"Hello, Adrian. Can I help you with something?"

The eager reporter swung the mike into his face. "Can you confirm you're searching for Horace Nelwin?"

"He's been missing for a couple of days, and we're checking on his whereabouts to make sure he's okay," said Corporal Fraser.

"I spoke to Horace Nelwin two nights ago and he said he was going to take a little trip over Maple Creek way for a few days." Adrian McDermott chuckled. "This wild goose chase will make a great story."

"What?" Todd stepped forward.

The reporter repeated himself as Craig moved up beside his brother, and Daniel stepped closer to the four of them.

"I don't get it," Craig said. "He told you, but not us?"

"That doesn't make any sense," Todd said. "Did he say why he was going?"

"I don't recall," the reporter shrugged.

"Where did you see him?" asked Craig.

"In the bar in town."

"That's a reliable place to hear things," Todd said sarcastically.

"Don't knock it. I hear all sorts of news there," said McDermott.

Todd gave McDermott a furious look and stomped away.

"Look, it's not my fault he doesn't let you know where he's going," McDermott said to Craig.

Craig shook his head in disgust and followed his brother to the house.

"I think you and I need to have a more in-depth talk," Corporal Fraser told McDermott. "Wait here."

Turning back to the search group, he said, "I guess we'll have to call off the search until I check out this story. Thanks for all your help. I'll be in touch."

Everyone dispersed quickly after that.

"He sure finds out about things quickly, doesn't he?" Dad said, joining Daniel and Doug.

"He seems to cover everything that goes on in the community, that's for sure," agreed Doug.

"Mom says he's way better than old Lorna Findlay used to be, anyway," Daniel said.

"That's for sure," said Doug. "She hardly ever left the newspaper office."

Doug went over to begin unsaddling his two trail horses. "It'll save me a trip later," he said.

Daniel and Dad helped him tie the horses behind his Jeep to take them home.

As they tied the final knots, Doug said, "What a life those boys lead. I feel sorry for them."

"You and me both," Dad said. "They're good kids. Horace doesn't deserve them."

Daniel realized again how lucky he was to have parents who cared about him. He couldn't imagine them leaving without telling him they were going somewhere, not even for a couple of hours. How empty and lost the Nelwin brothers must feel. Did he dare knock on their door and ask if they needed anything? Or had Todd had enough of him for one day? As he stood undecided, Dad took the decision away from him.

"You go home, Daniel. I'll make sure they're okay." He looked across the yard to the house. "Tell your mom I'll be back in a while."

Daniel nodded and swung onto Gypsy's back. He paused by Corporal Fraser's car, where the officer was standing talking on the radio. McDermott was gone. Daniel waited for him to finish his conversation.

"Uh, Corporal Fraser, I was just wondering if you'd made any progress on the *Stygimoloch* theft."

"Sorry, Daniel, nothing has come to light yet." He patted Gypsy's neck. "I'll let you know as soon as I find anything out."

"Thanks. I appreciate it," said Daniel. Trotting back home, he made good time and found Mr. Pederson and Mildred Roost waiting for him.

"I'll take care of your horse, young man," offered Dr.

Roost. "You go get your notebook and pictures; we have work to do."

Surprised, Daniel obeyed, not even questioning whether Mildred Roost knew anything about horses. He had assumed she didn't, but he could see from his bedroom window that she handled Gypsy as if she'd bred and raised horses all her life. Gypsy responded with measured ease.

From his bedroom closet, Daniel grabbed his backpack, still packed with the research he'd done the day before. He called to Mom across the yard, passing on Dad's message and letting her know he was leaving again.

"See you all at lunchtime," Mom waved from the garden where she was pulling cornstalks.

"Don't count on Ole and me," said Dr. Roost, "but Daniel will be back."

Daniel started to protest, but Dr. Roost shushed him. "We're only going to town to pick up supplies, once we figure out what we need."

"We're not going to exclude you on the plan making," Ole Pederson said gently. "We'll pool our ideas and see what we can come up with."

Mollified, Daniel asked, "Are you going for your doctor's appointment too?"

Pederson looked surprised. "How did you know about that?" He shook his head. "Never mind, no one can keep a secret for long around here."

"Should you be going into the past if something's wrong?" Daniel asked, his brows knitting in worry.

"It's nothing," Ole Pederson said. "Just a little checkup. I'm fine."

Dr. Roost shrugged her shoulders. "Not much is going to stop him."

When they reached Mr. Pederson's shack, they drew up a list of supplies, checking off those they had and noting those they needed to buy. Daniel explained his theories. They began a deep discussion about the merits of halothene, liquid nitrogen, novocaine and ether as ways to knock out a dinosaur.

"I do know that halothene takes quite a long time to wear off," said Pederson.

"Yes, the subject might wake up, but they still act sedated for hours," Dr. Roost agreed.

"We still don't know how much we'd need, or where to get it," Daniel piped up.

"I've used liquid nitrogen for preserving certain specimens. I might be able to get some shipped out from one of the museums," suggested Dr. Roost. "I'll make some enquiries on what it might take to sedate an elephant or rhinoceros and we'll calculate how much we'll need from there."

Daniel interrupted. "But how are you going to administer it?"

"Hmm." Pederson stroked his chin. "Good question. Injections and gas masks are obviously out." He smiled.

Daniel shook the image of a giant gas mask plastered over the mouth of a *T. rex* out of his mind. "What about some kind of a spraying apparatus?" he suggested.

As they mulled over the possibilities, they at last decided that a hand-pumped system might work.

"I already thought about that," said Daniel, "but a little motor or something like an oxygen tank gadget would be too heavy to transport."

"Maybe there's some kind of canister we could find that would explode like a hand grenade," Pederson offered.

"What about dry ice?" suggested Mildred Roost. "Dinosaurs are reptiles, after all, and they're cold-blooded, which means that as the temperature falls, so does their metabolism. If we could get the temperature cold enough around them, that would slow them right down."

"Not a bad idea, Mildred," said Pederson. "But again, how much would we need and how would we be able to apply it in this situation? They're not going to stand still while we pack it around them."

"And how quickly does it work?" added Daniel.

"Obviously we have a little research ahead of us," Pederson said. "How about we get started and see what we can find out."

"I had another thought. How about lasers?" Daniel suggested, though he hadn't finished the research on them.

"Great idea, Daniel," said Dr. Roost. "Ole, do you have any idea where we might get some?"

"Not at the moment, but let's get into town," Pederson suggested.

"We can start at the library and with the experts at the T. rex Discovery Centre. Surely we can figure out something," Dr. Roost said.

"We'll see what else we can find while we're there," said Pederson. He turned to Daniel. "Okay, lad, we'll drop you back off home for lunch and see you later."

Daniel felt a lump of disappointment settling in his throat. He wanted to go with them, but that obviously wasn't in their plans. Besides missing out on the action, he knew they'd go to Jack's Café, his favourite eating place.

Dr. Roost patted his hand. "We'll keep you posted on what we find out."

Daniel sighed. It wasn't what he wanted to hear, but it was better than nothing. The two of them were keeping tight with their plans. He knew it was because they worried about his safety, but still, he couldn't help feeling left out.

Several times throughout the afternoon, Daniel walked back over to Pederson's. But the truck was nowhere to be seen. Finally, on the last trip over, he thought to peer through a small window and noticed Dr. Roost's backpack and other gear on the table and he knew they still hadn't returned from town. Mildred would never have left her gear behind, so they hadn't hidden the truck somewhere as he was beginning to imagine. Even so, on his way home, he checked other locations he figured would be suitable for them to leave on a trip into the past.

But there was no evidence they'd returned home and gone again without him.

Surely they wouldn't chance going in the evening. He'd have to be up early, though, to catch them, if they were going in the morning. Maybe he was being too suspicious. They'd assured him they'd keep him posted.

But when he stopped to think about it, he realized Dr. Roost hadn't been specific about when she meant. Would they keep him posted about the results from their trip to town, or would they fill him in after they came back from the past?

By the time he headed for bed, the paleontologists had not returned. Were they deliberately excluding him? Had they already travelled without him so he couldn't tag along, even by accident? Daniel dropped uneasily off to sleep.

CHAPTER NINE

Daniel awoke very early the next morning to a quiet house and bright sunshine slipping through his blinds. Chickadees and sparrows chattered in the caragana hedge outside his open window. A breeze sent gentle puffs of cool air into his room. He breathed deeply and stretched, then rose quickly.

By the time he headed to the barn to do his chores, there was still no movement from anyone else. Only Dactyl padded up to him and pushed his head under Daniel's hand for some attention. Daniel quietly slid the huge door open and started his morning routine. The crispness of the early morning refreshed him.

After Daniel finished his chores and went back to the house, Mr. Pederson drove into the yard, but didn't stop. He waved to Daniel, who was standing at the kitchen window, from his old Studebaker truck and drove right up to Dr. Roost's vehicle. She opened her camper door and scuttled into his truck. He backed around and the pair disappeared out of the yard and down the gravel road in the direction of his shack.

Daniel sprinted up the stairs and grabbed his backpack. On his way out, he scrawled a note for Mom and Dad, saying he would be back in a while and that he would be with the two paleontologists. They weren't aware of it yet, but he had no intention of letting them get away from him.

Dashing across the yard to the corral, Daniel scrambled through the fence and whistled Gypsy over. His grey pinto mare whinnied as he clambered onto her bare back. Grabbing her mane, he rode her over to the gate, flung it open, and urged her through. Leaning over, he closed the gate and raced across the prairie towards the planned departure area. He didn't want to lose sight of Dr. Roost and Mr. Pederson.

As he cantered over the last hill on the way, he could see Mr. Pederson's truck bouncing across the rough terrain towards their destination. Daniel gave a light kick into Gypsy's side and she quickened to a gallop. So far, Pederson and Dr. Roost hadn't seen him. In fact, they weren't looking in his direction. When they ground to a halt, they hauled out their equipment quickly.

As they put on their backpacks, Daniel yelled, "Wait!"

But his voice was lost in the wind. Pounding across the ground towards them, he let out another holler. This time they looked up. He saw Dr. Roost grab Mr. Pederson's hand and nod to him. He plucked something out of his small notepad. Instantly, they were gone!

Daniel reined in and Gypsy came to a panting stop, her sides heaving.

"Good girl," he said, patting her as he slid to the ground.

Retrieving his notebook from his backpack, he commanded Gypsy to "Stay."

Gypsy snorted and began nibbling on the dry vegetation. She would be content until he returned. Daniel quickly moved to the exact spot where he'd last seen his two friends. He braced himself in anticipation of his journey through time. Opening his notebook, he snatched up his tiny branch. A whirling darkness engulfed him.

Seconds later, Daniel found himself on the verge of a clearing, several metres from where they'd landed on their last trip. He recognized some of the markings on the trees that he'd made on earlier visits. Watching constantly to make sure he was safe, he searched for Dr. Roost and Mr. Pederson along the edge of the trees. He spotted them quite some distance away to his left, standing back to back scanning their environment, looking a little like Hansel and Gretel trying to find their way.

He tucked the branch into his pocket and returned his notebook to his backpack, then crept closer to the pair. Every once in a while, Dr. Roost waved her cane to scare off huge flying insects. She seemed to be allowing Mr. Pederson to pursue his research while she kept watch.

As they moved around the perimeter of the open area, Daniel kept himself well hidden, but tried to remain not too far behind. The blood pulsed through his veins and his stomach felt like it held a piece of lead. Every nerve in his body tingled with fear. This really had to be the last time he travelled to the Cretaceous Period!

When he looked up, he saw that the sky was an unusual shade of grey, like dense smog hovering over a big city. Perhaps it was going to rain. Yet there were no dark cloud formations, just a wash of slate grey that covered the entire sky. He pushed forward, watching and listening.

He tried to ignore the shroud of grey as he followed the two adventurers, who stopped often to take photographs. Daniel couldn't believe how lucky they all were that no predators were about at the moment. Even sounds were muted and distant, as if this place was allowing them all to conduct a safe journey. But the air remained stifling hot and moist, and he began to have trouble breathing.

A foghornlike bellow burst through the stillness. Then answering calls. Hadrosaurs! Probably the herd of *Edmontosaurus Saskatchewanensis* they had seen before. All at once they burst through the trees. Daniel almost forgot all danger as he watched the incredible creatures forage for food along the edge of the meadow.

Moving on all fours, they twisted off lower twigs and bunches of conifer needles with their toothless beaks, passing the food into cheek pouches where hundreds of closely packed teeth ground it up. Daniel knew from previous research that *Edmontosaurus* were thought to have had sixty rows of teeth – eight hundred to over a thousand or so – but he didn't want to get any closer to count them. One of the biggest duckbills ever, they were almost twice the weight of a rhinoceros and more than four times the length.

The flat-headed creatures moved slowly across the open area, ripping at tough vegetation. From time to time, they stopped and adjusted their position to get a better idea of their environment. The older ones blew their cheek pouches, which created the loud foghorn bellow. The young hid behind the larger adults.

Now the whole environment seemed to awaken at once. A pandemonium of rustling and squeaks of small creatures skittering through the underbrush, along with the buzzing of oversized insects, filled the early morning air. Daniel wrestled off a small branch and waved it about, in case any of them decided to take a nibble of him. He became so intent on watching the ground, he forgot to look ahead and nearly plowed into a huge *Triceratops* grazing on low-lying plants. He'd done that before because, he supposed, they blended in so well with their surroundings. And they made very little noise except for rooting and the odd grunt.

He circled around it and momentarily lost sight of the old couple. When he saw them again, he was astounded to see they had crept into the meadow, closer to the hadrosaurs. He was ready to charge after them, when all of a sudden a *Stygimoloch* appeared. Followed by another and another. The small herd almost blocked his view of the hadrosaurs and of Dr. Roost and Mr. Pederson.

The plant-eating *Stygimoloch* stood alert on two legs, moving slowly like deer at the edge of a field. They were shorter than either Dr. Roost or Mr. Pederson and about two to three metres long. Their unusual domed skulls seemed to have some kind of thick covering that was a dark brown, compared to the light orangey-brown of its body. The skulls were adorned with three or four boney spikes, the largest about a hundred millimetres long. Several other knobs protruded around the nape of the neck.

Pederson shifted his attention from the hadrosaurs to the grazing *Stygimolochs* and began making notes on them, careful not to move too quickly. Even at this distance, Daniel could see the enthralled look on his face. Dr. Roost snapped photographs, not daring to go any closer.

Daniel found he was holding his breath. Creeping forward, he again checked for signs of peril. He peered up at the sky to look for pterodactyl-like creatures, but all he saw was the grey blanket that seemed to grow thicker as he pushed onward. When he was within a few metres of the action, he nestled down under a cycad and watched the *Stygimolochs* feeding.

He became fascinated by their small, curved, serrated teeth as they wrenched tufts of foliage from the ground and held it between their clawed, five-fingered hands. They ate quickly, only bending their heads to grab at their food, then standing upright as they munched, reminding him of kangaroos. He marvelled at how their stiff, heavy tails waved about in the air as they ate, balanced on long, powerful hind legs with three-fingered, clawed toes.

When Daniel looked up again, he noticed that the sky seemed even darker and specks of dirt seemed to be floating about, making breathing uncomfortable. Daniel reached for his bottled water to sooth his scratchy throat.

Other species joined those feeding in the meadow. Daniel wasn't sure what they all were, except that they were plant eaters. He did recognize *Thescelosaurus* and *Torosaurus,* and even an *Ankylosaurus* wandered through. Mostly the different species moved placidly near one another, oblivious to the other browsing groups. As they foraged, one of them would stop and take stock of their surroundings, perhaps startled by an unusual sound that might signal danger.

Mildred Roost seemed to be focused on the behaviour of the *Stygimoloch* herd. One of these small creatures always watched for predators and kept a short distance away from the others for clear sightlines. They also kept aloof from the hadrosaurs, paying them little attention as the herd made their way to the opposite side of the meadow. Daniel knew from experience that the

Stygimolochs were headed towards the river, their ritual watering hole.

As he advanced a little closer to the *Stygimolochs*, Pederson coughed. The watcher instantly became alert. Pederson stopped in mid-movement, both hands tight over his mouth, until the plant eater lowered its head and went back to grazing. Slowly, Pederson raised his binoculars. He seemed to be examining the beasts' hides.

As Daniel sat on the ground, he felt a little tremor. He kept his hand pressed to the earth and waited. Yes, there it was again. Something very large was approaching. He had to warn the others. Just as he stood up and was about to shout, the herds of *Edmontosaurus* and *Stygimolochs* began shifting uneasily. The hadrosaurs moved quickly and disappeared into the trees on the opposite side of the meadow.

Dr. Roost and Mr. Pederson noticed the change and stood on guard. They appeared not to know which direction to take, watching as the *Stygimolochs* moved towards the safety of the trees. Each creature would take a step, then check around for danger. Another step. Another check. Step. Check. Step. Check. One tentative step after another, they progressed back to where they had emerged. They were almost to the edge of the woods when the unmistakeable thunderous roar of a deadly *Tyrannosaurus rex* sounded. A sudden cacophony of noise reached almost deafening levels as various creatures rose to the sky or scrambled for safety, screeching and bellowing their warnings. The herbivores stampeded away, disappearing into the bush.

Dr. Roost and Mr. Pederson seemed to make an instant decision. They ran hand in hand, their gear pounding against them, following the lead of the *Stygimolochs*. When they reached the edge of the trees, they clung to one another, trying to see what was coming.

Daniel crouched beneath the cycad, trying to figure out where the *T. rex* was headed before he made a move. He didn't want to step into its path and accidentally find out if the theory about the *T. rex* having poor eyesight was right or not.

The crashing through the dense foliage became louder. All of a sudden, the deadly creature emerged only a few metres from where Pederson and Mildred Roost hid behind a tree. It swung and headed straight for the *Stygimoloch* herd. Mr. Pederson and Dr. Roost were in its path. They seemed to realize it at the same time.

They flung their backpacks off and drew out something that Daniel couldn't quite see. A bright light streaked across the meadow. Dr. Roost helped Pederson steady it and aim the powerful laser beam into the eyes of the *T. rex*. It roared as if in horrible pain, floundering until it came to a total stop, swivelling its huge head as if to shake away whatever was in its eyes. While Dr. Roost tried to keep the laser beam on the gigantic creature, Mr. Pederson drew something else out of their backpacks.

Moments later, Dr. Roost set the laser down and the pair of them donned hooded gas masks and grabbed canisters from the ground. They pulled at some kind of plugs at the top of the containers and threw them as hard as they could towards the disoriented creature. The *T. rex* continued to advance erratically, unaware of what direction it was headed. It gave another horrendous roar, drooling huge gobbets of saliva from between its long pointy teeth, which resembled deadly grass-cutting scythes. Its orange eyes glared like hazard lights from a semi barrelling down a highway towards them.

Mr. Pederson picked up the laser light again, but it was almost impossible to aim the beam while the *T. rex* jerked and heaved. He joined Dr. Roost, and they kept pitching canisters – maybe twenty in all. As they did so, they backed away as best as they could, ducking behind one tree after another, but the *T. rex* kept advancing in a crazed fashion. Daniel was powerless to help them. All he could do was watch in horror as the *Tyrannosaurus* staggered towards the old couple. Why didn't they drop the leaf or whatever vegetation they had and get back to the present? They seemed immobilized by terror.

"Drop your plant!" screamed Daniel.

They jerked around at the sound of his voice. Dr. Roost yanked on Ole's arm and they careened around a tree trunk and fell to their knees. Finally, the enraged beast seemed to be slowing down, but they had run out of ammunition. Then the creature roared again. Pederson dug frantically in his pockets.

All of a sudden, whatever was in the containers took effect. The *T. rex* froze and then crashed to the ground in slow motion. The echoes boomed over the landscape. The loud *Haru-u-umph-ph-ph* it exhaled as it hit the ground sounded like air escaping from a giant balloon. Its head lay only inches away from Dr. Roost and Mr. Pederson.

When Daniel was sure the creature wasn't moving, he raced towards them.

"No!" Dr. Roost yelled. "Don't come any closer. You don't have a mask!"

Daniel stopped in his tracks. While they righted themselves and staggered over to Daniel, he stared at the huge fallen beast. Barely heaving sides indicated it was still breathing, but Daniel wasn't sure how long the chemical would keep it immobile. They'd better get out of there fast.

When they reached Daniel, Dr. Roost was shivering, and as she drew off her mask, sweat streamed from her forehead. Ole Pederson trembled.

"That was a close one," he whispered, snatching at his gas mask and letting it hang around his neck.

"What were you thinking?" Daniel demanded, staring from one to the other.

"We wanted to see things up close and do what we could to save the *Stygimoloch* herd," Dr. Roost gasped out.

"At the cost of your own lives?" Daniel asked. "You two are crazier than I thought." Daniel realized he was sounding like he was their parent.

"I admit it was a dodgy decision," said Ole Pederson.

"Well, are you satisfied now? Can we all go home?" Daniel asked, gritting his teeth. Every fibre in his body vibrated.

Dr. Roost answered lightly. "Yes, I do believe we have enough notes and photographs of the *Stygimolochs*."

"Enough to work with for now," Mr. Pederson agreed. He paused for a moment until he had their full attention. "But this is a prime opportunity to study a *T. rex* up close." He motioned to the giant reptile.

Daniel and Dr. Roost stared at Ole Pederson as if he'd lost his mind. Daniel felt blood rushing into his head from the overload of adrenalin. Dr. Roost seemed to wrestle with her thoughts, while catching her breath.

"Sixty seconds, Ole," she gasped. "That's all the time you have. And I mean it. But you have to keep your safety gear on. The gas won't have dispersed yet."

He donned his gas mask, grabbed her camera and walked cautiously over to the downed *T. rex*. He took photographs from all angles, while Dr. Roost noted the time on her watch. She removed some of her gear and dropped it on the ground beside them.

Daniel stood helplessly by, scanning their surroundings and praying that no other vicious creatures would appear before Pederson finished. The darkening sky with bits of floating debris worried him too. He pulled the piece of branch from his pocket, ready to leave.

"Time's up!" Dr. Roost called.

Ole Pederson returned and handed the camera over to Dr. Roost's outstretched hand. He removed his mask and let it slip to the ground as he wiped his face.

Suddenly, Dr. Roost shrieked. "Oh no, not again!"

Daniel looked in the direction she pointed. A small pack of *Dromaeosaurus* vaulted towards them. Only half a metre high at the hips with sickle-like toe claws, sharp teeth and big eyes, the meat-eaters were considered very smart and would quickly surround the group, then move in for the kill.

"Okay, you two, time to go!" Daniel yelled.

Mildred Roost clutched Ole Pederson's arm as Daniel stared at them. "And you," he commanded Pederson. "Drop your plant, whatever it is!"

Mr. Pederson held his hand open with a flower blossom nestled in the palm. He glanced briefly at them both, then at the rapidly approaching pack of carnivores. With a shudder, he tipped his hand and let the flower slide away. At the same time, Daniel dropped his branch. Instant darkness engulfed them.

Daniel's ears hurt after they returned. His breathing hadn't quite returned to normal either, and his throat and lungs were sore. He sat down weakly on the ground. Pederson and Dr. Roost had landed nearby. For a moment, he couldn't even bear to look at them. The terror of almost losing them was more than he could handle. "Promise me you two won't ever do anything that crazy again!"

Dr. Roost smoothed out her clothes and cleared her throat, but she didn't say a word. Pederson coughed quietly, but didn't answer either.

"Did you two hear me?" he demanded.

"Yes," they both said meekly.

"Do you know how close we came to being torn to shreds?" he asked.

"Yes," Mr. Pederson answered feebly. Dr. Roost gave a faint nod.

Daniel realized he had to stop treating his friends like a couple of disobedient kids. He forced himself to take a few slow, deep breaths.

"Where did you get whatever it was in those canisters, anyway?" he asked.

"I have a friend who works at a zoo," Dr. Roost said gruffly. "Liquid nitrogen."

Daniel could feel the last of his energy draining away as his adrenalin levels dropped. "Can we call it quits now with the trips back to the past?" he asked.

They nodded. A haunting fear was still evident in their eyes. The three of them wearily gathered their gear.

Daniel whistled for Gypsy, not sure if she was still about or had returned home. She whinnied, though, from the other side of the hill and appeared within moments. He swung himself onto her back and loped home, leaving Mr. Pederson and Dr. Roost to return in his truck. Fatigue overcame Daniel, and he allowed Gypsy to pick her own way back as he slumped forward and rested on her neck.

He wanted to forget the whole ordeal, except that his mind kept mulling over the peculiar bleak skies in the past. The particles in the air behaved like fallout after a fire, although there hadn't been a burning smell, nor had he noticed any billowing clouds of smoke. The grey-covered sky was more solid and consistent, like a thick blanket. He would have to ask Dr. Roost and Mr. Pederson what they thought might have been the cause. For now, he just wanted to get home and be safe.

CHAPTER TEN

Daniel slid off of Gypsy near the corral gate, and settled her inside with a carrot and some fresh water. He'd revived somewhat during the ride home, but he shivered and headed to the house, where he found himself alone. He made himself a cup of tea. The hot liquid soothed his scratchy throat and warmed him up. While he drank it, he thought about their latest adventure.

Although Daniel wanted to talk to Mr. Pederson about the strange dome of darkness and the dark particles falling from the sky in the prehistoric world, he was surprised at the relief he suddenly felt that the old folks weren't joining them, and it confused him. He'd never before felt that he needed some distance from Mr. Pederson. Daniel considered how worried he'd been about Mr. Pederson lately and how much he'd miss him if anything ever happened to the old man. He recalled when the two of them first met a couple of winters ago.

Pederson had been anything but friendly – he'd warned Daniel to stay away from his land. He had made an important fossil discovery and wanted to keep Daniel away from it. Eventually, the old man got to know Daniel and warmed to his interest in paleontology. And then Daniel had rescued Mr. Pederson during a winter storm when the old man was very ill with bronchitis. Since then, Ole Pederson had mentored Daniel and the two of them had worked together on the *Edmontosaurus* project, Pederson's amazing discovery.

Daniel felt pride in his chest whenever the old paleontologist treated him like a colleague rather than a young boy. Pederson also was a little like Grandfather Bringham and Daniel had a very soft spot in his heart for the old paleontologist. He also realized that he'd expected Pederson would live forever, and that he'd been angry that the old man had jeopardized his life in prehistoric time.

All at once, Daniel felt lighter. The relief at figuring out the underlying reasons for the way he felt and how annoyed he had acted with Mr. Pederson and Dr. Roost had lifted a burden off him.

Daniel giggled to himself when he remembered the startled look on Pederson and Dr. Roost's faces when he ordered them home. Probably he should apologize to them both. For now, though, he was happy to have a break away from them. He needed to recover from the gruelling experience they had all just gone through. And though he wanted to discuss their trip with them, he could be patient.

A sudden rumbling from his stomach told him he was ready for food. He hadn't eaten breakfast before he left.

Daniel found his parents at the tourist campsite, where they were busy tidying up now that the season was over. Because they had the place to themselves, they'd decided to have a wiener roast for lunch. Daniel tucked into his food with pleasure and even helped Cheryl roast a marshmallow. Moments later, Dr. Roost and Mr. Pederson appeared at the top of the valley.

"Join us," Dad called, beckoning them.

"Thanks, but we're off to town," Dr. Roost hollered.

"See you later, then," Dad shouted. Daniel waved as the old couple turned to leave.

"Dad, has Horace Nelwin turned up yet?" he asked.

"No, though I believe the police are looking for him in Maple Creek. But I guess they figure he'll return home when he's ready," Dad answered, as Daniel helped him douse the cooking fire.

"And before you ask," Mom interjected, pulling on her gardening gloves, "no, there haven't been any developments on the theft of the *Stygimoloch*. Everyone is stymied."

"How can a grown man and a huge dinosaur fossil go missing so quickly and easily?" Daniel said, half to himself. "And why at the same time?"

"If we knew the answer, we would know a great deal more about everything going on around here," Dad responded.

"So Mom, do you want me to take Cheryl to the house for her nap or stay and help with the camp work?" Daniel knew Mom liked to be outside as much as possible.

"Neither," Mom laughed. "We're actually going into town to the bank as soon as we tidy up here. Do you want to come with us?"

Daniel's instant reaction was to say no, although he wouldn't mind knowing the outcome of their financial situation. "I think I'll just hang out here and see if we get any news," he answered. He hoped they wouldn't leave him with a whole bunch of work to do while they were gone. He didn't dare ask if they wanted him to do something.

"Sure," Dad said. "You could maybe help..."

Oh no, here it came. Daniel cringed.

"...Doug Lindstrom gather the last of his trail horses. He's coming over soon."

"That's it?" he finally asked.

"That's it!"

Whew. Daniel grinned. He'd gotten off easy.

"How about if I round them up now and move them to the corral, so it will be easier to gather them when he comes?" suggested Daniel.

Dad shrugged. "Sure, if you like."

"Did you want anything in town while we're there?" asked Mom.

"Just good news from the bank that we can continue our tour and dig operation," he said, smiling.

After his parents left, Daniel set about his task. The horses came as soon as he clanged on a feed pail. One by one, he put lead ropes on them and led them all at once to join Gypsy in the corral. Dactyl padded happily at his side as he worked. Daniel watered them all and left them to settle in, giving a little extra attention to his mare. As he patted Gypsy's nose, Daniel had a sudden flash of inspiration.

The search party for Horace Nelwin had been called off before they'd covered much ground. Although Daniel wasn't sure whether he believed that Horace Nelwin had gone to Maple Creek, he still wouldn't mind searching some of the back pastures, just in case he was out there somewhere. It would also give him the opportunity to look for the missing *Stygimoloch* skeleton. Along the way, he would stop in and see how the Nelwin brothers were doing. This time, though, he decided to saddle Gypsy so he'd be more comfortable.

Just as he finished placing all the riding gear on his mare, Doug Lindstrom arrived. Daniel guided him over to the horse pen. Within minutes, they tied the last of the horses to the back of Doug Lindstrom's Jeep and he drove out of the yard with them trotting behind. Moments later, Daniel mounted Gypsy and headed for the Nelwins.

Daniel found the two boys lounging on the back step of the house, using a slingshot to lob stones at an old tin pail, which they consistently hit. They barely acknowledged Daniel's presence, though they did order their dogs to lie down. Daniel dismounted and joined the boys on the step.

"No word yet?" he asked, sitting on the bottom rung.

"Nope," Craig answered, picking up another stone and flinging it. He couldn't tell if they were mad at him or just feeling depressed.

"Good one," Daniel said, when Craig's stone hit its mark. "Can I try?"

Craig passed him the slingshot. Daniel took careful aim and let it go. The stone walloped the ground in front of the pail.

"You need a little practice," said Todd, with an edge in his voice.

"Yup," Daniel agreed, handing the contraption back to Craig. He knew there was no point getting competitive with Todd. "I was just heading for a ride. Feel like joining me?" he asked.

"We only have the old nags in the barn," Todd answered.

"I'm not in any hurry," said Daniel.

Craig shrugged his shoulders. "Sure. Might as well go. Nothing better to do around here."

Daniel remembered Craig's interest in studying pale-ontology and thought of his recent adventures into the past. Would Craig like to go with him, if he needed to go again? Craig was already familiar with the environment. He'd keep the idea to himself for now.

Daniel waited on Gypsy as the pair sauntered off to saddle their horses. The warm sun beat down on him, making him wish he'd brought a cap. As if reading his mind, Craig reappeared and tossed a spare baseball cap at him.

"Thanks," Daniel said, shoving it on his head. Maybe they weren't mad at him. Craig, anyway. He wondered if either of them would have even thought of something like that before they started spending time at the Bringhams.

"Where did you have in mind?" Todd asked, astride his horse.

Daniel smiled.

"Let me guess," said Craig. "The rented pasture land."

"Right," Daniel said. "I've never been there before."

Todd did a little skitter with his horse, but gained control of it again, keeping his face poker straight. Obviously, Daniel had touched a nerve. It also told Daniel that even if Todd hadn't been involved with the theft, he suspected or knew something about it. As they rode across the first pasture, Daniel kept an eye on Todd's reactions. He might just lead them where they needed to go.

But as they sauntered along, Daniel realized Todd wasn't reacting in a way that indicated he had any knowledge of where they were heading. He didn't try to steer them in any particular direction. Todd couldn't possibly be involved with the theft! But maybe he was afraid his dad was and that this would cause some problems with working for the Bringhams. How could Daniel find out?

"So, Todd, did you manage to get whatever you needed straightened out the other day when you left our place early?"

"Not really," he said, his cheeks flushed a little.

"Is it anything I can help you with?" asked Daniel.

"Nope." He shook his head.

"Well, if I can help in any way, let me know," Daniel said.

Todd nodded, and seemed a little surprised at Daniel's offer. Then he prodded his horse and they caught up to Craig, who was examining a ravine.

As they rode, they heard the steady roar of a motor from somewhere in the distance, growing louder. Soon they made out the shape of someone on an ATV, bumping along as it sped across the rough terrain. Daniel wasn't sure what to make of it, though he could feel a churning in his stomach.

"I think it's Dad!" exclaimed Todd, leaning forward for a better look.

Craig exhaled loudly beside him.

Daniel didn't know whether to be elated that the man had returned or to prepare for something worse.

They reined in their horses. As the vehicle came closer, they could see Horace Nelwin at the wheel, unshaven and wild-looking with his hair matted and his clothes rumpled. Without even stopping, he shouted at them as he passed by.

"Get home! Those horses are for work, not for play!" He shook his fist at them and stepped on the gas as the ATV bounced over tufts of plants on the uneven ground.

Stunned, Craig and Todd stared after him for a few moments.

"This is not good!" said Craig, almost whispering.

"Better go," Todd urged, as he turned his horse around. "It'll only be worse if we make him wait."

Craig followed slowly behind him. "See you later, Daniel."

"Come to our place if you need help." Daniel said the only thing he could think of.

He knew there was no point in him going back with the Nelwin brothers to face their father. He'd only make things worse. The closest way home was by way of their yard, but he'd wait for a bit to give them an opportunity to get settled back at home. The first thing he'd do on his return was to let everyone know that Horace Nelwin had returned. At last, he clucked at Gypsy and they trotted off.

As he passed through the Nelwins' yard, he could hear Horace yelling at his sons in the barn. Before he could escape, the angry man crashed out and rammed the sliding door shut. Daniel tensed when Horace caught sight of him.

"Just stay away from here!" he shouted. He shook his fist and stomped to the house. The dogs barked loudly from inside the barn.

Shaken, Daniel rode out of the yard at a quick pace and arrived home a short time later to a yard empty of vehicles and people. The silence settled around him as he unsaddled Gypsy and put her back in the corral with some fresh water. He liked being on his own, but he was bursting to tell someone about the return of Horace Nelwin. He paced the kitchen floor trying to decide if he should wait for his parents to return, but he had no idea when that would be. At last, he picked up the phone and dialled Corporal Fraser's number. Although he wasn't in his office, Daniel managed to call his cell phone and deliver the news.

"I'm nearby," the RCMP officer relayed. "I'll pay a visit to the Nelwins." He paused. "And before you ask, Daniel, no, there are no new developments on the theft. But we'll see what Horace Nelwin has to say."

"Thanks, Corporal Fraser."

Daniel hung up the phone and opened the fridge, looking for a snack. He made himself a peanut butter and homemade raspberry jam sandwich and followed it with a tall glass of cool milk.

The first to arrive back were Mr. Pederson and Dr. Roost. They drove right on by the house and Dr. Roost got out at her truck and was inside her camper before Daniel even had the back door open. He stepped outside and waved Ole Pederson down. The old man brought the truck to a halt and rolled down the window with an expectant look.

"Uh, Mr. Pederson, do you have a minute to talk?" Daniel asked, looking up at the kindly face.

"I think I can spare some time for my wise young friend," replied Pederson, giving Daniel a smile that crinkled the corner of his eyes. "I'm just happy you're speaking to me again," he added, lightly.

Daniel grinned back. "I could never stay mad at you long."

"How about making a foolish old man a cup of tea?"

"Coming right up!"

Daniel ran to the house, where he plugged in the kettle and rummaged around until he found some leftover peach pie and a carton of ice cream. As he set out the dishes and made tea, Daniel told Ole Pederson about Horace Nelwin's return.

"Corporal Fraser's probably over there talking to him right now." Daniel relayed their encounter. "I don't think he was in Maple Creek like Adrian McDermott told us, since he was travelling on his ATV."

"I doubt it too. Those things aren't that comfortable to go that distance," agreed Pederson, sipping his tea. "That newspaper reporter must have been mistaken."

As they devoured the pie and ice cream, their conversation changed to a discussion of their trip, comparing notes and sharing their observations.

"What fine specimens of *Stygimolochs*," Pederson said. "How lucky we were to observe them."

"But how are you going to be able to use the information?"

"That is a concern." Pederson's whole body drooped a little. "I'm not sure yet, especially without the fossils to study. Even though I have first-hand knowledge, I can't divulge anything without referring to the *Stygimoloch* bones."

"Surely the fossils will turn up sometime," Daniel said.

"I hope so. In the meantime, I can certainly analyze what I have in preparation for when we get our skeleton back." Pederson spoke with a little more spark.

"It's only been a few days since the theft," said Daniel. "We just need to be patient," he added more for his own benefit than for Mr. Pederson.

"True. Now that the RCMP has been making enquiries that are more specific and it's been spread throughout the community, we can get the public's help. Maybe start an in-depth search of the area," Pederson said.

Daniel turned the conversation back to prehistoric time.

"Did you notice the sky in the past?" he asked. "Do you think it was a storm coming, or was there maybe smoke from a fire in the area?"

"I think it was something much more than that, lad," said Pederson. He fell silent, stirring the spoon in his cup, as if stalling for time.

"What?"

"I almost don't want to say it."

Daniel felt the hairs on the nape of his neck rise as a sudden thought came to him.

"I think it might have been volcanic ash. I was nearby when Mount St. Helens erupted and the atmosphere was very similar."

"But I didn't think we had volcanoes in this area." Daniel racked his brain to remember what he'd read.

"I doubt that we did, at least not many," Pederson explained. "But, over eons, there have been some horrendously big ones, like the one millions of years ago in what is now India. Scientists believe some of the major ones spewed ash, pumice and carbon dioxide that covered more than half the world. So we might have been seeing the effects of one."

"Isn't that what they think lead to the extinction of the dinosaurs and other life?" Daniel asked.

"That's one theory," said Pederson, "but the more popular one is..."

"Meteorites or asteroids hitting the earth," finished Daniel. "I'm not sure what I believe."

"More evidence recently is supporting the meteorite theory," Pederson said, "and that could also have caused the dark cloud and the particles we saw in the area."

"What do *you* think happened?" Daniel asked.

"I suspect it was a combination of many things. The effects of the volcanoes produced major climate changes to the land and to the oceans," said Pederson. "Then the massive meteor bombardment came along, which changed the entire world once and for all."

Daniel thought about that for a few moments. "I was reading on the Internet about the enormous craters researchers have discovered all over the world."

"Yes, some of the most famous are in North America, Mexico and Australia. They suspect they were made when the huge meteorites and asteroids hit the earth," Pederson explained. "And when they compare the geological evidence of the time when the craters were made, it seems to coincide with the time of the extinction of the dinosaurs."

Daniel whistled, imagining the destruction. "That really must have been something back then."

"Yes, it was catastrophic. Nearly seventy percent of all the species on Earth and much of the life on the planet was wiped out, not just the dinosaurs," said Pederson. "It was one of the worst worldwide disasters ever."

"You mean there was more than one that wiped out life?" asked Daniel.

"There have been many, although only five are considered major," Pederson answered.

"But the one sixty-five million years ago is the most famous one," Daniel said.

Pederson nodded.

"Amazing." Daniel tried to imagine what it would be like if it happened on earth now. Everything would be gone.

Pederson sat up straighter.

"But you know, Daniel, the shower of meteorites didn't just drop from the sky one day and kill everything all at once. The process happened over thousands and millions of years."

"Really?" said Daniel. "I guess I never realized that."

"Most people don't," said Pederson, as his eyes grew brighter. "It's actually a very slow process. Especially when you consider humans have only been around for about three hundred thousand years."

"That's no time at all compared to the history of the earth," Daniel said. "But look what we humans are doing to the world now."

Pederson nodded his head. "True, but we can't blame *all* the global climate problems on the way humans have treated the world. There is a natural cycle that occurs on the planet over millions of years, and things from the atmosphere that affect it as well, which have created the many global warming disasters throughout geological history. Many think those earlier global warming episodes were created by volcanic ash."

"How did that work?" asked Daniel.

Pederson leaned forward. "Well, the volcanic ash freely allowed the sunlight to enter the earth's atmosphere to heat the surface, but it trapped a great deal of the heat that is normally reflected back into space."

"So everything overheated," said Daniel.

"Yes, and that raised sea temperatures and killed off many marine species as well as much of the plant and animal life on land," added Pederson. "The problem right now is that we humans are causing an even worse problem by producing too many harmful gases that are trapped in the atmosphere."

"So that they're stopping the normal gases from going back into space, and we're over heating the planet?" Daniel asked.

"Yes, at an alarming rate."

"And that's why they call it the greenhouse effect?" asked Daniel.

Pederson nodded. "And if we humans aren't careful, we'll create another major global warming disaster."

"And that could result in another massive extinction – including us," Daniel said.

"Yes, and the human race is already headed in that direction," Pederson said. "Look at how dry our weather is in this area of the province. If we don't get enough rain in the next couple of decades, nothing will be able to live here. In other areas there is flooding because the polar ice caps are melting and causing water levels to rise all over the earth. And there are instances of strange weather behaviour everywhere on the planet."

"But there are things we can do to stop the destruction of earth this time," said Daniel.

Pederson agreed. "But it's almost too late. I'm glad I won't be here in another fifty years' time to see what's happened to our environment."

Thoughtfully Daniel said, "And then there are all the problems of overusing or abusing other natural resources. That can cause habitats to die and then species can't find food. And this adds to the possibility of a major disaster for mankind, right?"

"Uh-huh." Pederson tilted his head, considering Daniel's comments. "Destruction of rain forests, pollution of drinking water sources and damage to the land where we live is causing a lot of damage."

"Just like the dumping of that leaky oil barrel," said Daniel. He shuddered, thinking about the oil spill in the ditch less than a mile away. Whoever it was may not even have noticed the barrel falling off his truck, and it was used oil, which was even worse. Although only a minor near disaster, an accident like this contributed to the world's problems.

"True, lad," said Pederson.

Daniel decided to see if he and his family could make more of an effort towards saving the environment with their everyday practices. Living on the farm made it easier than for his relatives in the city, who had to drive a vehicle every day to work, shop and carry on their regular activities, which created harmful amounts of gas emissions.

His family didn't need to travel much. They grew most of their own food in a healthy way and recycled or reused almost everything they handled, and they only drove to town or anywhere when they absolutely needed to go. They were as self-sufficient as they could be, using natural resources in a limited way, and carefully disposing of garbage and other waste. They didn't use pesticides or other harmful chemicals on their farm, and they had a plentiful well on their property. Daniel was sure there were other things they could do to improve their practices. They could also do more to spread awareness and let others know about things they could do.

Right then, Daniel had an idea of what career path he wanted to take. Besides studying the field of paleontology that he so dearly loved, maybe he could do more than look at the past. Maybe he could combine knowledge of prehistoric times with environmental science to help keep the world a healthy place to live, so that mankind would not become extinct like the dinosaurs.

"What I *would* like to see is what's going on in the Cretaceous Period right now," said Pederson, bringing Daniel's attention back to the present.

Daniel held his breath, hoping Pederson wasn't thinking what he thought he was thinking. And then he said it.

"What we saw might just have been the start of the dinosaur extinction. Wouldn't it be fabulous to know what really happened?" Pederson sighed, as he drifted into quiet thought.

Daniel didn't respond. He tensed, waiting for Mr. Pederson's next suggestion. He hoped his friend wouldn't want to go back to the Cretaceous Period to investigate.

"You know, Daniel," Pederson finally focused on him, "If we had a way of going again..."

"No way! Don't even talk about it!" Daniel warned him, jumping up. "That would be way too risky, even if we had a way! Which we don't!" He crossed his fingers behind his back. He'd actually gathered another leaf secretly, but didn't want to let on. He'd only use it for an urgent situation. And he couldn't imagine what that would be.

"I suppose you're right," Pederson admitted hastily. "Well, I guess I'd best be off."

He rose and took his dishes to the kitchen sink. Daniel did the same, but he watched Mr. Pederson closely, not convinced the old man had dropped the idea entirely. He had responded a little too quickly and with no complaints. Daniel couldn't figure out how he'd transport himself back in time, since he'd made Mr. Pederson drop the flower. Did he have something else hidden away, just as Daniel did?

CHAPTER ELEVEN

Daniel decided to watch Ole Pederson to make sure the paleontologist wasn't planning any more trips to prehistoric time. Maybe he could get Dr. Roost's help – he was convinced she didn't want to go again after their last scare. He headed over to her truck and knocked tentatively on her camper door. Rustlings and then a thump came from inside. A moment later, she swung the door open.

"Daniel, I'd invite you in, but it's a little cramped in here." She stepped outside. "What can I do for you?"

He told her his concern. Dr. Roost agreed. "Yes, if he has a way to go, I'm almost sure he will."

"Maybe he has a way," Daniel said. "He could easily have stuffed a leaf or something in his backpack.

"That's what I'm thinking," Dr. Roost said.

"He's on his way home now, and I hope he isn't planning to go right away," Daniel said, shuffling his feet.

"He'll need to gather a few more bits of gear before he goes again."

"Do you think I should go check?"

"Nope, I don't," said Mildred Roost. "The excitement from this morning will have tuckered him out. My guess is he won't go to town to stock up until morning. That is, if our suspicions are correct."

"And the stores don't open until later." Daniel nodded in relief. He could maybe have a good night's sleep for a change, free of worry.

"No, *they* don't, but the museums and gas stations do, and that's where he needs to go."

Dr. Roost's comment brought Daniel out of his complacency. He groaned.

"What kind of stuff would he be getting?" Daniel asked.

"Well, the laser lights didn't work as well as we'd hoped," she said. "He mentioned taking a little container of gasoline in case he needed to make a small fire in a hurry. Most creatures are afraid of fire, so probably the large ferocious dinosaurs will be too." Dr. Roost squinted in thought. "I suspect his contacts at one of the museums will give him a chemical that he could use as an anaesthetic. Who knows what ideas he'll come up with?"

After some thought, Dr. Roost said, "He may have to travel farther than he thinks to get what he needs. We cleaned out most of the supplies locally." Then she added, "The good news is that we don't have to follow him around, just keep a watch on him when he returns."

"We'll know when he returns, because his truck will be there," Daniel said, "But how will we know when he's going to go to the past?"

"I'll see if I can get him to confide in me," she said.

Daniel raised an eyebrow. "Does that mean you'll end up in cahoots with him and leave me behind again?"

Dr. Roost chuckled. "No, I honestly don't want to go again, Daniel. My heart couldn't take it."

"You have a bad heart and you didn't say anything!" Daniel scolded.

She shook her head. "I didn't mean it literally. I just mean the excitement and danger is more than I want to deal with again."

Daniel exhaled loudly. "Thank heavens!"

"Don't get me wrong," she added. "I love seeing and being part of prehistoric time, but I agree it's simply too difficult to concentrate much on research with all the hazards. I don't like worrying about being eaten by some horrific creature with vicious claws and giant serrated teeth, or stomped to death accidentally like an insect!"

"We're in agreement on that at least!" Daniel said. "So how should we organize looking out for Mr. Pederson?"

"How about if I pop over there shortly and see what he's up to and if I can find out when he's going to town?" Mildred Roost suggested. "Then I'll come back and report to you and we'll make our plans."

"Sounds good," said Daniel. "Thanks."

"You're welcome, young man!" she said. "Besides, you were right, I do have a soft spot for Ole Pederson and I don't want to see him get injured doing something foolish. We have a few years left in us yet to spend some time together. And to share our paleontological studies."

Daniel smiled, a feeling of warmth spreading through him. "I want him around for a long time to come too."

"Off with you then. I have some work to do," she ordered with a cheery smile.

As Daniel headed back to the house, he heard her rummaging around in the back of the truck camper, and then the slam of the camper door. Moments later, the truck door slammed, and the motor started. Mildred Roost gunned out of the yard, waving heartily at him as she passed. She barely stopped before she barrelled onto the gravel road, just as Daniel's family were about to turn into the yard.

Daniel met them in the yard, released Cheryl from her car seat, and carried her into the house. Once he'd plopped her safely in her high chair, he helped carry in the groceries and other supplies. At the same time, he told them about Horace Nelwin's return.

"I guess all we can do is wait and see if Corporal Fraser is able to tell us anything more about Horace Nelwin's mysterious movements. It doesn't sound like the man is likely to tell us himself," Dad said.

"That's one thing we can be sure of," Mom sighed.

"Even if where he's been maybe isn't any of our business, I'd like to know if he was involved in any way with the theft," Daniel said. Mom and Dad stopped what they were doing and looked at Daniel. Then they chuckled.

"So, you've been having the same thoughts," Dad said, shaking his head.

"He seems the only logical person," Daniel answered.

"It would explain why he was gone at the same time as the disappearance of the fossils and why he's been away so long," Mom said.

"It would also explain why no one has been able to find the fossils around here. He's probably taken them much farther away," Dad added.

"Wait a moment. We don't know for sure that Horace is even involved," said Mom.

Daniel kept his thoughts to himself, but he had a hunch that the fossils were close by. He just needed a little time to explore. He'd start by checking the rented pasture land. With Dr. Roost checking on Mr. Pederson, maybe he should go before it was time for chores and supper.

"Do you mind if I go for a ride on Gypsy?" Daniel asked, crossing his fingers behind his back again. "Or do you have something else you want me to do?"

Mom and Dad looked at each other and shrugged their shoulders.

"Nope, you're free till chore time," Dad said, smiling.

Hastily, Daniel saddled Gypsy and headed towards the Nelwins, with some trepidation. Going through their property was the only way he knew to access the rented pasture. His plan was to ask politely to cross their place, if he ran into Old Man Nelwin. If that didn't work, he'd have to go to the Milners' who lived next to the Nelwins and get directions, but he didn't want anyone to know where he was going. Dactyl trotted along happily beside him.

By chance, he found the Nelwin farmyard empty and everything quiet. Even their dogs had disappeared, which was good, because he didn't want Dactyl attacked. The truck was also missing, so Daniel supposed they'd gone to town or something. He hurried through the yard, then made good time getting to the fence that divided the Nelwins' place from the rental property.

Finding a way into the pasture took a while, but at last he found a piece of fence that was down and was able to cross over. There was a faint trail of old packed-down grass, so others must have used it some time far in the past.

Daniel didn't know where the supposed ruins of the old buildings were located, so he took a zigzag tack across the rolling hills of the pasture. The landscape was burned brown, with drying clumps of tumbleweed, late wild daisies and sagebrush. Gypsy avoided hidden gopher holes and cactus plants with experienced ease as the late afternoon autumn sun cascaded down on them.

Dactyl disappeared and reappeared several times, chasing gophers and nosing about as Daniel loped along, thankful that he lived where he did. He had the best of everything with his home, his pets, the country life and the chance to search for prehistoric fossils. He wrapped his reins around the saddle horn and let Gypsy wander at will, as he settled back, taking in his surroundings. In a lower section of the meadow, a soft breeze rippled foxtails like waves on a gentle sea. Meadowlarks and red-winged black birds fluted at them as he swung past low bushes and a small stand of poplar trees.

Daniel pulled out a pair of binoculars he'd brought with him and studied the horizon. During his second sweep, he noticed a heap of grey boards some distance away. He nudged Gypsy in that direction, guessing it was the old Collins homestead site. When he came closer, he picked up the reins again.

Cantering over, Daniel found what was left of a long-deserted pioneer shack that leaned precariously toward the ground on one side. He slid off his horse and wandered around the tumbledown structure on foot. Dactyl joined him and nosed around the boards looking for mice.

One side of the old house had caved in on itself. It was nothing but a pile of boards that weather must have battered for half a century. The rest of the tattered boards were buckled, held up by a single rotting roof beam. He couldn't see how anything much could be hidden within it.

As Daniel peered into the dilapidated structure through some gaping, weathered one-by-eights, his eyes slowly adjusted to the darkness inside. From the mote-filled beams of sunlight that filtered into the ramshackle structure, he stared into the area where everything had collapsed into what must have been a root cellar. He saw an old bed frame, pieces of a rotting old cupboard, a few cracked dishes and more signs of wreckage that had fallen through decaying floorboards.

He supposed the family must have been small if they'd only had one bed. He pulled at a crumbling board to get a better look, and could just make out a faded brown photograph wedged into a crack in a timber. A couple with a small child on the mother's lap sat stoically on a bench outside what Daniel guessed was this very house. They must have gone in a hurry if they'd left so many of their household belongings behind. Had they been forced off their land because of the Great Depression in the 1930s?

He could imagine the land being even dryer than it was this year, so dry for years that gaping cracks erupted and the earth became too hard to grow crops or a garden. He could see the family desperate without rain, leaving everything behind in despair, with only the clothes on their backs, walking along the dusty road trying to hitch a ride anywhere away from their desolate life.

Disappointed at not finding anything of use, Daniel gathered Gypsy's reins and prepared to climb back up and head for home. Then Dactyl gave a sudden bark.

"Here boy," Daniel called. "Time to go."

Dactyl barked again, but Daniel couldn't see him.

"Here Dactyl," he called again. Then he realized that Dactyl's bark was coming from within the fallen-down structure. How had the dog gotten in? Daniel walked around the place again, until he found the opening Dactyl must have used. Peering inside, he urged Dactyl to come out, but the dog seemed to have something cornered and didn't want to leave.

Staring into the gloom, Daniel suddenly noticed what looked like a pile of old clothing stashed in an opposite corner from the long-forgotten household goods that had fallen into the root cellar. A thought struck him. He tried to pry the boards apart to get a better look, but the mouldering planks had more strength than he expected. He found a rock and pounded the boards until one broke. Ripping fragments off with his hands, he poked his head inside and waited for the dust to clear and his eyes to adjust to the dim light.

As he studied the heap of old clothing, he gasped. There they were! The jacketed *Stygimoloch* fossils, hidden under the old clothes. Daniel had almost missed seeing them. But how did whoever stole the bones get them in there? Transporting them to the decaying shack without anyone hearing or seeing was maybe the easier part. It was miles away from anywhere, but the fossil pieces were big and needed a large opening to wrestle them inside.

Daniel searched for signs of entry into the rubble heap. The first time around, he couldn't see anything. But the second time, he noticed some sweeping marks on the ground, as if someone had tried to hide tire tracks and footprints by using a branch to mess up the dirt. Then he saw where the boards had been disturbed.

Peering through them, he saw an exterior entrance to the root cellar that had been covered up by the caved-in boards. He called Dactyl out in a voice that demanded he come *now*. Dactyl obeyed. Not wanting to disturb anything in case he was messing up evidence that would lead to the thieves, Daniel raced over to Gypsy.

Moments later, he galloped across the rolling hills to find a phone. Not only did he not want to pass through the Nelwins' place again, but there was no point in going there when they didn't have a phone. Also, he still figured Horace Nelwin might have had something to do with the thefts and there was no way he wanted him to know his suspicions. He'd never been to the Milners' from the back pasture before, but he headed cross-country in the general direction until he came to a gate that he figured must lead to their farmyard.

He arrived amid a kafuffle of dogs greeting him and Dactyl in a friendly manner. Herb Milner stepped out of his machine shop with a welcoming smile.

"Could I use your phone?" Daniel asked, breathing hard.

"Sure thing, Daniel. Is something wrong?"

"I think I've found the fossils." He couldn't keep the excitement out of his voice.

"That's great news!" Herb Milner invited him into the house. Daniel tethered Gypsy to a caragana bush, told Dactyl to lie down and followed him inside.

"The rest of the family is in town," he said, showing Daniel where the phone was. "I'll be back in the shop when you're finished. Let me know if you need me for anything." He left Daniel alone to make his call.

Daniel hastily called home, but there was no answer. They must be outside. He dialled the cell phone number instead. Dad answered. Quickly, he explained the situation.

"I'll call Corporal Fraser," said Dad. "You stay where you are. We'll meet you."

"See you soon, then," Daniel said.

When he wandered back outside, Daniel heard Herb Milner clanging on something in his machine shop. He checked on Gypsy and was surprised to note that Mr. Milner had kindly given her a pail of water. Dactyl shared it with her.

As Daniel headed to the machine shop, he heard the roar of a vehicle on the gravel road. He looked up just in time to see Dr. Roost whiz by, returning from Ole Pederson's place.

As he stood wondering what she had discovered, Dr. Roost suddenly screeched to a halt, just as Dad met her from the other direction. They spoke for a few minutes as the gravel dust whirled around them, then Dad drove on towards the Milners'. Dr. Roost ground her gears as she backed around and took off again in the other direction, probably on her way back to Ole Pederson's to tell him the news.

By this time, Herb Milner poked his head out of his shop. Before Daniel could say a word, Dad drove into the yard on their ATV. Seconds later, Corporal Fraser's RCMP car followed Dad down the winding, tree-lined approach.

Herb Milner took off his hat and scratched his head. "You sure can cause a lot of action, Daniel," he said.

Daniel grinned.

Dad and Corporal Fraser walked over to Daniel and Herb Milner. "Now, young man, let's hear what you found," suggested Corporal Fraser. Quickly, Daniel told them.

"Whose property is it now?" Corporal Fraser asked.

"I own it, though I've rented it to Abe Johnson as pasture," Milner said. "But you're welcome to search it any time."

"I appreciate your help, Herb," said Corporal Fraser. "Mind us crossing your land to get there?"

"Not at all. There's a good trail through, shorter than the way Daniel came."

"Thanks," said Corporal Fraser. He called headquarters and put them on the alert.

Daniel mounted Gypsy and Corporal Fraser hopped on the ATV with Dad. Following Milner's directions, they arrived at the dilapidated shack within minutes, although the police officer did ask Dad to slow down from time to time to check out tracks. Daniel showed them what he'd found, pointing out the spots where he'd looked, including the entrance to the root cellar.

"It looks like the fossils are there all right." Corporal Fraser shone his heavy duty flashlight into the darkness of the cellar. The strong beam clearly revealed the lumps of jacketed bones. Dactyl scampered back inside, but Daniel quickly ordered his pet out again.

Dad spoke to Daniel quietly. "Well, son, it seems you've done what no one else could. Good work!"

"Thanks, Dad," Daniel said. "But it was actually Dactyl that found them."

"Maybe, but how did you figure they could be here in the first place?" asked Dad.

"Just a hunch," Daniel replied. "A couple of people mentioned the place in passing, but no one seemed to consider it worth looking at."

"It is rather a good hiding place," Dad said.

Corporal Fraser used his cell phone to confirm the need for the camera and lab equipment, giving them directions to the Milners' farm.

"I can go back and lead them here," Daniel offered, excited to be part of retrieving the fossils.

"I'll go back too, if you don't need the ATV, Corporal," said Dad. "I think we'll need some tools to clear some of this debris away and some other equipment to winch the fossils out of there."

Corporal Fraser agreed. "But you'll need to wait until we've done the forensic investigation before you can move the pieces," he said.

"Sure thing," Dad answered. "It's going to take a while to gather a trailer and winches and ropes, not to mention a tractor to lift them out of that deep cellar. And maybe someone to guide the ropes or chains."

"Yes, it was much easier for them to get the pieces down there," said Corporal Fraser. "All they had to do was tip the trailer and basically let them fall in."

Daniel winced at the thought of the damage that must have been done when they rolled and hit the ground.

"Good thing this is a much smaller dinosaur than a *T. rex*," said Dad. The pieces were anywhere from a metre and a half to two metres across, but awkward and heavy with the jackets protecting them.

"I just hope they're not too broken up," said Daniel, going over to stare down the hole again.

"We'll know soon enough," said Dad, as he hopped back on his ATV. "I'll take Dactyl home with me."

Daniel gave him a quick wave and climbed onto Gypsy. When he left, Corporal Fraser was busy taking measurements and jotting in his notebook.

CHAPTER TWELVE

While Dad continued home, Daniel waited in the Milners' yard. As he told Mr. Milner what they'd found, another vehicle appeared bringing their conversation to a halt. Mildred Roost had arrived.

She hobbled over to Daniel and Herb Milner, using her cane to propel her. "Did you really find the stolen *Stygimoloch*?" Dr. Roost's eyes looked wild with excitement.

"Yes!" Daniel brought her up to date.

"What was Mr. Pederson's reaction when you let him know?" Daniel asked

"I didn't get a chance to tell him." Dr. Roost sounded exasperated. "He wasn't there when I went back. He'd already left for Swift Current."

Mr. Milner had a mild look of interest on his face. Daniel wanted to know more about Pederson's plans too, but didn't want to ask in front of Mr. Milner.

"Oh, getting those paleontology supplies we needed," Daniel said.

"Right," Dr. Roost agreed. "So what can I do?"

Daniel explained that they were waiting for the forensics team.

"I'd like to take a look too," she said.

"I can guide you there when I take them," Daniel offered.

"Fine," she said. "I'll just make sure I have my camera in my truck."

Suddenly, the sound of a speeding vehicle reached the peacefulness of the Milner yard.

"Adrian McDermott, I bet!" Dr. Roost said. "How that man knows things so quickly is beyond me."

Herb Milner moved up beside Dr. Roost. "He sure has a 'nose for news,' as they say."

"Yes, and we can't stall him any more about this story now that several people in the community know about the fossil theft," she commented, as the reporter parked his car beside her truck.

"Especially since he already seemed to be aware of the situation the other day when he showed up at our place," said Daniel.

Herb Milner stepped forward with a concerned look on his face. "Obviously he has some kind of inside source."

"Yes, but I wonder who?" Daniel asked.

"We could ask him," suggested Mildred Roost with a chuckle, as the young man strode towards them with his tape recorder and microphone in hand.

"Good afternoon," Adrian McDermott said, smiling. "So I hear the dinosaur fossils have been found in an abandoned farmyard. What can you tell me about the location?" he turned to Herb Milner.

Mr. Milner pointed to Daniel. "He's the young fellow that found them," he said.

"All right!" The reporter turned his attention to Daniel. "So what can you tell me about how you found the jacketed pieces?"

"Boy, you sure know a lot already," Daniel said, surprised.

"I have my sources," said the reporter cheerfully.

"Like what?" Daniel asked curiously.

"Listening to the police band on the Internet," McDermott answered lightly.

Daniel hadn't known this was possible, but it certainly explained how McDermott always seemed to know what was going on. After a moment of surprise, Daniel explained how he'd been riding through the pasture and Dactyl had delayed him long enough to make the discovery.

"What condition are they in?" McDermott asked.

"We don't know yet," answered Daniel. "The police are still checking out the site."

"That's fine then, Daniel," said McDermott with a little laugh. "I'll just head over there and take some photographs."

Herb Milner stepped forward. "I don't think that's a good idea while the police are carrying out their investigation," he said. "How about you wait around with the rest of us here?"

"Uh, thanks anyway," McDermott said, stepping back to his car at a quicker pace than he'd arrived. "But I have other things to do. I'll maybe come back."

Dr. Roost and Herb Milner watched as he reversed and then pulled out of the yard.

"Quite the ambitious young man," declared Herb Milner.

"Yes, he certainly keeps abreast of what's going on," said Dr. Roost.

Daniel wished he knew what was going on with the Nelwin brothers, especially Todd. As soon as he could, he'd confront the brothers once and for all to see why they were being so secretive and if it had something to do with their dad being involved with the theft.

He also wanted to get the scoop from Dr. Roost on what was going on with Mr. Pederson. Obviously if he'd gone to town for supplies, he had another way to go back to the past. But now was not the time to quiz Dr. Roost.

Wielding her cane over her head, Dr. Roost said, "I want to be ready. I'm not missing this action. Wish we didn't have to wait for the forensics crew, though."

"No problem," Milner said, pointing to a cloud of dust approaching in the distance. "Here they come."

A few minutes later, Daniel was leading Dr. Roost and the forensic team across the pasture.

As soon as they arrived at the falling-down shack, Corporal Fraser gave the forensic officers directions. A few minutes later, Daniel and Dr. Roost stood chatting with him. They mentioned Adrian McDermott's visit.

"I think its time to question Mr. McDermott about his information gathering methods. I'm not sure if he's a help or a hindrance, but we might need to set down some guidelines for him," he said, then headed back to where the squad of officers squatted near the opening to the root cellar, taking photographs and making notes.

Daniel led Dr. Roost some distance away from hearing of the crew. "Mr. Pederson's going to go back again, isn't he?" Daniel asked.

"I'm afraid so." She poked her cane at some old boards in the tall grass. "I tried earlier to convince him otherwise, but he wouldn't listen."

"When?"

She grimaced. "He wouldn't tell me."

"I knew he'd brought something more back from the past with him," said Daniel.

"I'm sure he'll be too tired to go before morning, especially if he's got to go all the way to Swift Current to get supplies," she consoled him. "He told me he wasn't going there until tomorrow, but when I went back to tell him you'd found the *Stygimoloch* skeleton, he'd already left."

Daniel sighed. At least they had a little more time before they had to take up their guard duty on Mr. Pederson. "Too bad he doesn't know the bones are safe, otherwise I'm sure he wouldn't want to travel back in time again."

"You might be right." Mildred Roost didn't look entirely convinced.

"After all," said Daniel, "losing them was the reason we went in the first place."

"True," agreed Dr. Roost.

Daniel knew Mr. Pederson wouldn't have returned from Swift Current yet, but Daniel would go to his place as soon as he thought his friend might be home. He didn't want Pederson going back into that kind of danger, especially not with the added concern of the grey blanket that hung heavily in the skies and the falling debris in the atmosphere.

If what Ole Pederson said was true, Daniel knew that the dinosaurs they'd visited didn't have much time to live. Besides the trapped heat that warmed the planet too much for life to survive, the vast ash cloud they'd witnessed would block the sunlight for years and prevent photosynthesis, which was the way plants made food. This would mean the gradual extinction of land and aquatic plants, which in turn meant there would be no food for any of the living things in the Cretaceous Period that depended on them – including the dinosaurs.

There were also other dangers. Carbon dioxide was naturally present in the earth's atmosphere, and was needed to help plants grow. But too much would kill them. Sulphur gases and other atmospheric elements, including iridium, and carbon monoxide produced by volcanic activity, would be devastating to most life forms. Daniel didn't like the thought of Mr. Pederson going to the past and possibly inhaling some of those deadly chemicals.

When Dad arrived with some tools for making the removal of the boards easier, Daniel jumped at the chance to help. Together he and Dad pounded out rusted nails and pulled rotting boards out of the way for the police team, heaving them onto a pile a few metres away. Soon the entry to the root cellar was easily accessible.

The police team signalled for Daniel and Dr. Roost to come down and check the contents. The jacketed pieces were scratched and dirty on the outside, but as far as they could tell, the large fossils inside were intact, saved by the thickness of the plaster coating over the layers of tissue paper and burlap underneath. The smaller pieces hadn't fared as well. Many were broken and dumped into a mound all jumbled together.

Dr. Roost let out a low sigh almost like a moan. "Realigning these will take many painstaking hours of work."

"At least we still have them," said Daniel.

"It will certainly keep Ole busy all winter," she said.

"Speaking of which," Daniel lowered his voice, "do you think he's back yet?"

She looked at her watch. "It's a bit early yet. Give it another half hour or so." She poked her cane into the ground. "Well, there's nothing more for me to do here. Guess I might as well pop over to Ole's and wait for him so I can give him the news."

"Great!" said Daniel, finally able to smile.

"Are you staying?"

"Yes, I want to watch them hoist the fossils to safety."

"Where are they transporting them?"

"They'll store them in our garage for now – it can be locked – and Dactyl will keep guard in the yard. We'll hear him bark," explained Daniel. "Then they'll see what Mr. Pederson wants to do with them. I know he wanted them to go to the Royal Saskatchewan Museum eventually, but I don't know if they were to go to the field station at Eastend or the Regina headquarters."

"Sounds like things are well in hand. See you later, young man!" Dr. Roost gave him a tap with her cane.

Daniel watched the tractors, flatbed and other equipment arrive, along with several other men in trucks, including Herb Milner, and someone on a horse. Although they struggled at first to lever the fossils to haul them out, once they had a system in place, the whole operation went fairly quickly. Seeing them in daylight, they found the plaster of Paris jackets were in worse shape than they'd hoped. As Daniel had expected, some were cracked and badly banged up, because the thieves had rolled them into the root cellar without worrying about how they landed.

"Someone sure didn't know what they were doing," said Dad. "Or how valuable these pieces were."

"They didn't care about destroying other possible finds at the quarry, either," said Daniel saddened by the destruction. "I still don't understand why anyone would do it."

"They wanted to hurt us in some way, I suppose," Dad said. "Though why, I wouldn't know."

When they were almost finished loading the pieces, Daniel happened to catch a flash of bright light from across the pasture. He pulled out his binoculars and watched carefully. When it happened again, he pinpointed the place and studied it. At last, he saw other movement and realized it was someone with a telephoto lens on a camera, reflecting in the sun. Whoever it was crept closer on foot, attempting to hide behind bits of scrubby sagebrush and small bushes.

Daniel sidled over to Corporal Fraser, handed him the binoculars and indicated with a slow nod for him to look at the glinting in the distance. Corporal Fraser moved behind a protruding chunk of debris and studied the area.

"Adrian McDermott," guessed Daniel.

"Yes, I do believe it is," answered Corporal Fraser. "Now, how do you suppose he knew where to find us? Most people only know of the two ways of getting in here. I definitely need to pay that man a visit sometime soon and find out what he knows from his 'sources.'"

Daniel took the binoculars back from Corporal Fraser, who went back to finish supervising the task of gathering the smaller pieces. When they were ready to leave, Daniel at first rode slowly behind the caravan of Jeeps, ATVs, tractors and flatbed led by Corporal Fraser. But Gypsy seemed ready for another good run, so he galloped across the hills. Partway across the pasture, he doubled back to the site of the old falling-down shack.

He surprised Adrian McDermott, who was taking photographs of the site. McDermott tried to run and hide when he heard Daniel coming, but he was no match for Gypsy's speed. Besides, he had nowhere to hide where Daniel couldn't find him.

"What do you think you're doing?" Daniel demanded, drawing up beside him.

"Getting my story on the missing *Stygimoloch*," Adrian McDermott said.

"How did you get here?" asked Daniel, knowing he hadn't come by either of the two usual routes.

"I'm good at my job and I do my research." The reporter turned smug.

Daniel suddenly remembered Adrian McDermott telling someone he was doing a project on old abandoned places. He must have found another way in.

"And just how do you know so much about what's going on here?" Daniel circled Gypsy around the reporter.

"I told you, I have my sources." The reporter relaxed a little.

"What sources? No outsiders know about the *Stygimoloch*," Daniel insisted, brushing closer to McDermott. "Let's hear about them."

"Yes, let's," said the voice of Corporal Fraser, suddenly stepping out from the pile of weathered boards.

Daniel let out a little yelp. He hadn't heard Corporal Fraser's return. He must have looped back around on a borrowed horse. McDermott tensed, his eyes became wary. He gave a quick glance around, looking for a way to escape.

"I don't have to tell you anything!" he retorted.

"I think your knowledge has nothing to do with protecting the sources for your story," said Corporal Fraser, moving closer to McDermott. "I insist you join me right now for a little chat."

McDermott seemed to wither. He sighed and returned his camera to the bag. "Fine," he said.

"Daniel, how about you head for home and I'll drop by in a while," suggested the Corporal.

Daniel nodded, giving McDermott one last piercing look. Corporal Fraser would get the truth from the reporter. Daniel turned Gypsy around and headed for home. Maybe the Nelwin brothers were there by now.

He was just in time to see the flatbed backed securely into the garage. Everyone congratulated themselves on a job well done and disappeared from the yard in a short time. Daniel cooled Gypsy down and stabled her with fresh water and her evening feed. Then he did his barn chores.

He kept looking through the open barn doors, hoping to see the Nelwins arrive, but they never did. His desire to ask Todd what he might know about his father's possible involvement in the theft was not going to be satisfied that night. Dad came to help him finish the chores and together they returned to the house for supper.

Daniel was just about to head for bed later that night, when he finally heard Dr. Roost arrive back in their yard. He scurried over to her parked truck and knocked on her camper door. She stepped out, greeting Daniel with discouragement in her eyes.

"Ole still hasn't returned," she said. "I checked a few of the spots in case he took a sudden desire to go into the past tonight, but I'm sure he hasn't gone yet. Something must have held him up in town. I didn't want to wait for him all night, so I left him a note pinned to his door," explained Dr. Roost. "I told him the fossils had been found."

"I guess there's nothing more we can do," Daniel said. "He surely won't want to go when it's dark."

"I'll take first watch in the morning," said Dr. Roost. "That way you can get your chores done."

"Okay," Daniel agreed, although he hated to miss a moment of keeping watch over Ole Pederson.

Daniel said good night and sauntered back to the house, staring up at the night sky and the constellations. He easily picked out the Big Dipper and Orion's Belt. How much had the stars changed over sixty-five million years, he wondered? Had the Cretaceous dinosaurs lived under the same formations? He supposed the constellations must have appeared to have changed position each time a major natural geographical disaster shifted the Earth's axis – at least that's what the scientists seemed to believe.

Later, Daniel readied his backpack for the next day's jaunt to watch over Ole Pederson. He checked his notebook to make sure the leaf was secure, then tucked it into his backpack in the closet, before setting his alarm for four a.m. He didn't trust Ole Pederson not to leave by daybreak. The old man always rose early and Daniel didn't know if Dr. Roost would get there fast enough.

When he finished packing his camera, binoculars and a dinosaur book to study, he snuck downstairs. There he readied his jacket and shoes by the back door, making sure he could easily grab some bottles of water from the fridge when he left. Back in his room, he didn't even get into his pyjamas, not wanting to disturb anyone when he got up. Before he crawled into bed, he checked again to make sure the recently picked prehistoric leaf was secure in his notebook.

Sometime during the night, the wind picked up and rain brushed against the windows. There was still a slow drizzle blown about by a strong wind when Daniel rose. Luckily his rain gear was stored in the porch and he had little trouble finding his poncho and rubber boots. He tucked his sneakers into his backpack for later. He'd let Dr. Roost take over the watch when he left to do chores.

The sky was dark and dreary as Daniel headed over the rolling hills to Mr. Pederson's shack. He ordered Dactyl to stay home and the dog seemed contented to obey, curling back up in his sleeping spot on some soft straw in the barn just inside the partially open door. Using a flashlight, Daniel stumbled over the uneven ground until the sky lightened to a softer grey and the rain diminished to a few drops now and then.

From several hills away, Daniel could make out the speck of Mr. Pederson's roofline a little farther down the valley. He pulled out the binoculars. Mr. Pederson's truck was parked close to the shack. Daniel relaxed. Mr. Pederson was home.

Then he noticed movement and gasped. The old paleontologist was carrying some object from the back of his truck and placing it on something oblong that lay on the ground. Daniel began to run. He lost sight of Pederson when he dipped down into a valley. Panting by the time he made the next rise, he studied the action below.

"No!" he yelled when he saw what Pederson was doing. He was still too far away to stop him and there was no way the old man could hear him over the fury of the wind.

Pederson continued to haul items from his truck, but he was placing them on an inflated rubber dinghy! What looked like ropes and tackle, then a fair-sized canister of something, a spraying machine, a backpack, camera equipment, and other things that Daniel couldn't quite make out, were stacked evenly at both ends. When the oars were added, Daniel knew Pederson was going to try to land in the river. But what if he didn't hit the right spot? The dinghy could be overturned, or he could land on the shore. Worse, one of the meat-eating dinosaurs could be having an early morning drink and Mr. Pederson would be a goner. Daniel didn't even want to think about the creatures lurking in the water.

Daniel pounded across the next hill and raced towards Pederson. But the paleontologist still couldn't hear or see him. He was intent on donning some kind of overalls and a full-face mask hooked to a small oxygen tank strapped on his back. Frantically, Daniel charged across the top of the last hill and down towards Pederson, waving his arms and yelling. He dug a whistle out of his pocket and began blowing as hard as he could.

Pederson saw him then, but didn't stop. Instead, he hopped into the dinghy, sat down, and grabbed the oars. Then he picked up something on the seat beside him. A split second later, he was gone.

CHAPTER THIRTEEN

"**N**o!" Daniel yelled and kept running.

When he reached the spot where Pederson had disappeared, Daniel hurriedly drew copies of the two area maps out of his backpack. The wind lashed at them as he tried to figure out how he could join Pederson in the past without landing in the river. He didn't want to be breakfast for meat-eating marine reptiles like the *Mosasaurs* or the three-metre crocodile *Borealosuchus,* nor did he want to be scooped up by an *Ichthyornis* – a powerful seabird with a lower jaw that held at least twenty teeth.

But if he didn't hurry, Pederson might be swept far down the river and into the sea before he arrived. He decided he needed to be a few metres up the hill above Pederson's shack, which he hoped would land him on the bank above the river. He pounded his way back uphill, slipping on the rain-soaked grass. Struggling against the wind, with the rain striking his face, he stuffed his maps into his backpack and then dove for his notebook.

Without a moment's hesitation, he grasped his pre-historic leaf.

Daniel found himself standing on a crumbling piece of the riverbank in almost complete blackness, with wind-whipped hair in his face and raindrops dripping from his forehead. He scrambled for a better footing and clung to a pine tree, terrified he was exposed prey. He gasped, trying to catch his breath, but bits of something caught in his throat. He swiped his hand across his face to clear the moisture from his field of vision and scoured the dismal, dark location.

At first, he thought the sun had not yet risen.

Then he realized falling debris shrouded the whole environment. He was in the middle of some kind of geological fallout! He wrestled for his water bottle and took big gulps to wash out his mouth and throat. He shrugged out of his poncho and yanked off his T-shirt. Pulling his jacket out of his backpack, he put it on with the rain poncho overtop. Wrapping his T-shirt around his head, he covered his mouth and nose. Next, he pulled his cap down as far as it would go to shield his eyes from grit. The most important thing was to find Mr. Pederson and get back home!

He moved towards the river. There was a weird stillness in the air and he felt prickles creeping up the back of his neck. The atmosphere had changed rapidly since his last visit. Cloying heat made it difficult to breathe, and his entire body felt clammy. He wouldn't last long without a proper mask with some oxygen. He couldn't go back to the present and get one; it would take too long.

Suddenly, he remembered the masks and other equipment that Dr. Roost and Mr. Pederson had left behind during the *Dromaeosaurus* attack. If he could get to the spot, he'd be fine until he could locate Pederson. He surveyed his surroundings and compared them to the map he'd made, trying to work out where he was. He plotted a route he hoped would lead him to the equipment he needed. He'd have to brave the open meadow to shorten the jaunt both going and returning. And he'd have to be fast.

Daniel jogged through the jungle-like terrain, his t-shirt over his mouth, being careful not to trip over vines and large-leafed vegetation. Howling and shrieking surrounded him in the peculiar darkness. His lungs hurt and his heart pumped hard, but he carried on.

When he came to the edge of the meadow, he found *Edmontosaurus*, *Stegoceras*, *Thescelosaurus* and *Stygimoloch* rummaging for food. He paused for a moment to catch his breath, watching as they nibbled at dust-covered, crumbling leaves and other decayed plants. Some trees had turned black.

Daniel was astonished to see the creatures all at once turn on one other, nipping and biting, panicked by the rapid changes around them. Daniel heard their terrified screeches, saw the bleeding wounds on their bodies.

There was no way he was going to be able to go across the meadow.

He swerved to his left, figuring that was the closest way to the mask and other oxygen tanks. Underfoot, slight tremors made running difficult. He shut out his thoughts, concentrating on moving as fast as he could, yet watching for imminent danger.

Suddenly, a horrific roar resounded, followed by vicious snarling that made him go weak. He dived under a cycad to get his bearings, as the hideous sounds of two huge dinosaurs fighting grew louder.

Then there was a sudden moment of quiet.

He was about to venture over to the next giant fern, when a terrible crashing of trees and branches came from his right and two *Tyrannosaurus* flashed into sight. They lunged at each other, propelling themselves into the open meadow, gaining momentum as their fight intensified. Thrusting massive tails, they plunged forward, biting into one another's leathery hides, leaving deep gashes streaming with blood. Snarling ferociously, one suddenly smashed his head against the other's throat. With a loud snap, one *T. rex* sank to the ground with a final dreadful scream. The other gave a fierce roar of triumph.

Daniel stayed frozen, not knowing what to expect next. He'd forgotten to keep watch on the herbivores, but when he looked, they'd disappeared, more intent on saving themselves from the *T. rex*.

Cautiously, Daniel crept as quickly as he could away from the carrion meat-eater, which was already ripping flesh from its fallen opponent. He needed to give it as much distance as possible. Everywhere there was pandemonium. Creatures he'd seen previously were acting in peculiar ways and the sky turned ever darker, filling with tumultuous clouds of black particles and thick dust.

All of a sudden, a lump of glaring light sizzled towards the ground some distance away. When the burning object hit the ground, sparks flew many metres into the air and cinders rained over a huge area. Rumblings sounded in the distance like thunder, and the earth still rumbled beneath his feet. Daniel had no idea what was causing all the disruptions on the earth. All he knew was that he needed to find Pederson and get both of them home to safety!

He sprinted as fast as he could to the area where the masks should be. If he'd guessed right, he was close. And then he saw them. He grabbed one, then threw it away. It was damaged beyond repair. Some big creature must have stepped on it. He rummaged through the rest of the belongings, and finally uncovered the second mask. Pulling his T-shirt away from his face, he drew on the mask and adjusted it snugly, slung the small oxygen container in its carrying harness onto his back and plugged the hose into the mask. It worked! He took several deep breaths and felt his lungs ease. Without taking time to do up all the straps on the harness, he reversed direction and raced towards Pederson – or where he hoped he was.

He made it back to the riverbank unscathed, except for his horror at the devastation around him. He skirted an *Ankylosaurus* and a *Triceratops*, pawing for food in the blackened vegetation. He narrowly missed stepping on a cat-sized *Purgatorius*, but for the most part he tried not to dwell on the perplexing state of the animals or his own danger. Otherwise he would become paralyzed with fear. He concentrated on finding Pederson instead.

Struggling down the steep embankment, he searched for the edge of the river by following the sounds of lapping water. He tripped on something and almost fell. He looked down – it was the back end of a shell from some tortoise-like creature, probably a *Basilemys*. The thick, brown-spotted casing was one and a half metres across, covered with a layer of silt. Daniel skirted the creature, avoiding the head in case it snapped at him. He wasn't sure how fast it could move, so he gave it a wide berth.

Frantically, he tried to get his bearings, wiping moisture from his face. The temperature had risen and he was uncomfortably hot, but he didn't dare take any of his clothing off. Was the heat caused by the descent of a burning meteorite shower, or the results of hot volcanic lava and ash spewing thousands of kilometres away?

At last, Daniel made it to the riverbank. Had he heard the sound of oars paddling in water? He listened intently, afraid to call to Pederson for fear of attracting some kind of menace. He peered through the dark haze and saw what looked like the shadowy form of Pederson floating along in his dinghy several metres to his right. But the image faded and he was sure he'd only imagined it.

Daniel could now see that a layer of black particles covered the entire river like melted cheese on a bowl of French onion soup. Debris from trees, plants and soil floated on the top like toasted croutons. Whether these substances came from volcanic ash or some kind of dust from a meteorite he didn't know. Either way, a thick residue covered the entire landscape and there didn't seem to be any end in sight to the particles cascading down.

Farther down the shore, he could see what looked like the shorebird *Cimolopteryx*, its brightly coloured body covered with a grey film of dust, cackling and flapping its wings as it tried to shake itself clear. Around a bend, on higher ground, a small group of *Corythosaurus* pawed at the layer of powder covering the dying vegetation, searching for food. Daniel knew it would only be a matter of time before the food became scarce and the landscape insufficient to sustain life as the plants died off.

As he stumbled along the river's edge, Daniel found breathing difficult. A weird smell like rotten eggs filled the air, likely sulphur gas. His hands felt clammy and his eyes stung. He tried not to rub them and almost had to close them. His eyesight was limited to an area smaller than that of a vision slit on a medieval knight's helmet with his visor pulled down ready for battle. He only wished he had a full suit of protective gear and infrared binoculars or a spotlight to find Ole Pederson.

Daniel continued along the riverbank, keeping a watchful eye for predators, including any *Pterosaurs* that might be invading the skies above him and meat-eaters trolling for quarry. He made his way slowly down the shore, still following what he thought was the sound of paddles rustling in water.

Over the river, a flock of *Ichthyornis* screamed their dismay, sounding more forceful than the present-day terns they resembled. On the bank, *Cimolopteryx* probed in the mud for food with their long, slender bills. And out on the river a lonely *Hesperornis* swam through the gunk covering the water, searching for tiny sea creatures.

Daniel figured the fierce-looking prehistoric shore-birds posed no more threat than those in current times, but he wasn't sure if the giant bees that alighted on small flowers would attack him. He felt reasonably safe with the dragonflies – they'd ignored him before and he didn't have time to worry about tiny ground creatures.

He tried to shove down the panic rising from the pit of his stomach. His mind churned with questions about how his surrounding environment was affecting him. Who knew what lethal substances fell all around him or what harmful gases filled the air? He had no protection against anything floating in the air even though he wore an oxygen mask. Maybe he'd die along with everything else.

Hopelessness engulfed Daniel as he realized there was nothing he could do about the cycle of extinction. Eighty to ninety per cent of the Cretaceous life he had experienced would die. Not just the individuals in front of him, but whole animal species and most of the plant life. He had no way to influence or stop the devastating horror.

All he could hope to do was locate Pederson and bring him home.

Ahead, Daniel caught sight of an unusually large mound along the riverbank. As he moved closer, he realized this was the place where he'd found the injured *Edmontosaurus* on his other trips. Now a mound of earth covered her, the result of the embankment collapsing when two *T. rex* fought to their death above her. He could almost make out the outlines of her body, curled protectively around a nest. He remembered her twisted hindquarter and broken forearm that made it impossible to survive or fend for her young.

But what had happened to her hatchling that Daniel had rescued? In the increasing darkness and swirling debris, Daniel searched for the grass and earth enclosure he'd fashioned for the baby *Edmontosaurus*. And then he saw it. A fine layer of dust particles covered the little body. Its leathery sides barely moved and the little pouches by its nose hardly expanded. Daniel knelt and tenderly brushed some of the debris off its body, but there was no movement beneath his hand. Sadness welled up when he realized it had stopped breathing. He covered it gently with earth.

Suddenly he heard coughing coming from some distance down the river. It had to be Pederson! He followed the sounds in the murkiness, sure now he was going in the right direction. The sound of oars pulling through water was stronger and Daniel started to run.

He lifted his mask and called cautiously, "Mr. Pederson?"

The rowing stopped. The coughing continued.

Cupping his hands to his mouth, he called louder. "Mr. Pederson."

"Daniel?" said a rough, rasping voice.

"Yes." Daniel moved closer. "Mr. Pederson, I'm over here."

A loud bellowing came from somewhere behind Daniel, and then a tortured squeal.

"Over here," Daniel yelled, guiding Pederson to him. "Come quick." He pulled his mask back over his mouth.

He had never been in the past when it was dark before. He had no idea what was out there beyond his field of vision, which wasn't more than a few metres. The thought of a huge *Triceratops* or an *Edmontosaurus* stepping on him by accident almost made him faint. Flying reptiles circled closer. Although many were fish-eating, the sharp teeth in their beaks still made his legs feel weak.

Then he reached Mr. Pederson.

With the swirling mass of debris in the dark foreign landscape, Daniel felt like he was on some other planet staring at an astronaut in a pressure suit. Pederson wore some kind of environmental overalls with a full-face oxygen mask and protective headgear. He pulled the dinghy closer to shore.

"What are you doing here?" Pederson demanded, briefly removing his oxygen mask.

"What are *you* doing here?" Daniel challenged.

Daniel stepped towards the water's edge, replacing his mask. His boots were instantly sucked into the gooey mud. Grabbing the rope that Pederson threw him, Daniel tugged on it, dragging the dinghy onto the beach. On wobbly legs, Pederson stepped out and Daniel helped him manoeuvre through the muck.

"Why did you come?" Daniel demanded.

"I wanted to do further research on the *Stygimoloch* and its environment," Pederson answered innocently.

"But why, when you knew the fossils had been recovered?"

"You found them?" Pederson seemed stunned by the news.

"You didn't know? But Dr. Roost left you a note on your door."

Pederson shook his head. "I didn't see it."

Daniel groaned.

Pederson shrugged. "Well, it's been an interesting adventure. I'm glad I came."

Obviously holding back a tickling cough in his throat, Pederson motioned to Daniel to pull the dinghy farther onto the shore.

"We may need the other equipment," he wheezed, beneath his mask.

"It's too dangerous to stay here," Daniel warned, but he did Pederson's bidding.

"It certainly is for you without any proper protective gear!" Pederson cleared his throat.

As Daniel turned back to Mr. Pederson, he froze.

"Don't move," he mouthed.

Pederson stood stock still. Lurking in a stand of trees over the riverbank was a huge, vicious head with glaring yellow eyes. As it swung around, Daniel saw dozens of razor-sharp teeth in its mouth. Another *Tyrannosaurus*! Their only hope was to keep still.

As he waited for the *T. rex* to leave, the blood rushed into Daniel's head until the pulsating was so loud, he almost couldn't stand it. When the *T. rex* gave a deafening roar, Daniel wanted to cover his ears but didn't dare move a muscle. He had no idea how long the ferocious meat-eater had been watching them. He hadn't heard it arrive. Maybe it had been there all the time and the two of them had disturbed its sleep.

After several tortuous minutes, the humungous creature gave another terrifying swivel of its massive head and gargantuan jaws and lumbered off. Trees and branches cracked and snapped under the weight of its body.

Ole Pederson sat heavily on the ground. Daniel walked over and sank down beside him.

"Can we go home now?" Daniel asked.

"Well, I do have some marvellous specimens," Pederson said hesitantly.

Daniel suddenly found breathing difficult. He sucked harder on his oxygen line, then began to gasp. He realized he was out of air!

Pederson noticed instantly, plucked his oxygen mask off, and passed it to Daniel. Daniel took several deep breaths, then returned it to Pederson, who sucked on the mouthpiece and inhaled between sputtering coughs. Daniel removed his useless mask and tank, discarding them on the blackened riverbank.

"We need to get you back into air that's safe to breath." Pederson took another deep breath, then handed it back to Daniel.

"Okay, let's go," Daniel agreed, fearing for Pederson's health. He also worried about his own safety, especially as they had to share the oxygen. They continued to pass it back and forth as they talked.

"You go, Daniel," said Pederson, patting his arm and stifling a cough. "I want to do a couple more things."

"Like what?" Daniel asked in dismay.

"I've been investigating the aquatic life, floating down the river and getting a quick overview of this location, but now I'd like a higher perspective." He pulled a handkerchief out of his pocket and held it over his mouth.

"Don't tell me you want to climb a tree?" Daniel stared at the tall trees surrounding them. Their lowest branches were several metres off the ground.

"It will be a perfect vantage point," Pederson said. "Besides, I have the equipment to do it."

"Equipment?"

"Drag that dinghy over here. I have all kinds of gear in it," said Pederson.

Daniel pulled his T-shirt over the bottom half of his face and dragged an armload of ropes and pulleys out of the rubber raft.

"See?" Pederson said, coughing. "Now you can go home and I'll be along in a bit."

"I'm not leaving without you. Besides, you can't do it on your own."

"Yes, I can. I'll pull myself up." As they shared the oxygen mask, Pederson outlined his plan to hoist himself up with a pulley and harness.

"How are you going to get the rope up to a high enough branch, even if you could pull yourself up?" Daniel pointed to a stand of tall pine and redwood with massive trunks.

"Throw it." Pederson shrugged.

Daniel stared, incredulous. Pederson was pale and wheezing, and obviously too weak to throw the rope to any height.

Daniel shook his head. "There's no way you can do it. And I'm not strong enough either. Those trees are impossible for me to climb too."

"I'd really like to accomplish this. It's the last thing I'll do." Pederson said half-serious and half-joking.

"It might be, if we don't get you home," retorted Daniel.

"This is the chance of a lifetime." He looked from Daniel to the trees and back again.

"Don't you want to live to enjoy what you've already accomplished?" Daniel asked, wiping the sweat from his face, accepting another round of oxygen. "We can't stay here any longer. You're already worn out."

"I'm fine, lad," said Pederson, but he couldn't hide his trembling limbs or shaky hands.

"We need to go home." Daniel begged. "Please!"

All of a sudden Pederson's eyes widened as he stared at something behind Daniel.

"Look," Pederson whispered.

Daniel turned to see a swelling grey-black cloud in the distance. Beside him, Pederson began clicking away with his camera. Daniel watched, mesmerized as the billowing dust and debris expanded over the landscape. Then the rising wind caught the massive swirl and it rolled and boiled towards them. A twisting funnel-shaped cloud appeared.

"Let's get out of here!" Daniel yelled, grabbing Pederson's arm with one hand, while he pulled the prehistoric leaf out of his pocket with the other.

As they took turns sucking on the oxygen, Pederson struggled to find his piece of vegetation in one of the pockets of his overalls. Daniel's body vibrated with desperate terror as he helped Pederson search. The old man seemed to become disoriented, moving slowly between bouts of coughing. Sweat ran down both their faces.

At last, Pederson drew out his large leaf with trembling hands. He nodded at Daniel, then grabbed for his backpack. They took one last look at the swirling mass of dark debris, heard the horrible shrieks of the wind and the terror of the creatures, then they stared into each other's eyes. Together they dropped the bits of plant material that had brought them so far into the past.

CHAPTER FOURTEEN

They collapsed where they landed on the hillside above Pederson's shack, gasping fresh, clean air. Daniel helped Pederson drop the oxygen mask and tank on the ground. For several moments they lay quietly in the early morning autumn sun. At first the silence seemed deafening, but gradually sounds emerged. Wind rustling the dried grasses, the call of an occasional songbird, the chatter of a gopher nearby and the distant clatter of a combine in a field somewhere.

Daniel clutched at the grass beneath him as the adrenalin drained away, leaving him weak as a newborn calf. He removed his poncho and other gear, laying it on the ground beside him. He was in no hurry to stand up and move.

Pederson struggled to a sitting position, wheezing and coughing, and trying to pull off his outer clothing to cool himself down. Daniel helped him remove the protective suit.

"Are you going to be okay?" Daniel asked.

Pederson's face had turned red from the effort to gain control of his breath and his eyes watered. As the coughing subsided, he nodded feebly and lay back down. Lines of fatigue etched his pale face and his breathing was shallow and raspy. He closed his eyes, too exhausted to move.

Alarmed, Daniel stood up. "I'm going for help."

Pederson gave no indication that he'd heard. Daniel felt a jolt of panic from his toes to the top of his scalp. He had to get to a phone. Pederson's shack wasn't equipped with one, but maybe the cell phone he used for tours was there. Daniel pounded down the hill, almost tripping over a grassy hummock in his hurry.

Reaching the dilapidated shack, he flung the door open and crashed through the doorway. He searched for the phone, scattering papers from the table and checking pockets in clothing. He couldn't find it. Just as he got down on his hands and knees to check under the bed and dresser, a vehicle screeched to a halt outside the door. Daniel rushed outside to find Dr. Roost getting out of her truck.

"Daniel, what's happened?" Dr. Roost hurried towards him. "You look like you've been dragged through the mud!"

When she reached Daniel, she gave him a little shake. "Don't tell me you've been back in the past again!"

Teeth chattering, he nodded.

"Was Ole there too?" she demanded.

"Yes," Daniel spluttered. "That's why I went."

"What's wrong?"

"It's Mr. Pederson. He's not moving. We need an ambulance." Daniel couldn't keep the tremor out of his voice. He pointed up the hillside to where Pederson lay in the grass.

Dr. Roost raced to her truck and grabbed something from the glove compartment. She handed Daniel a cell phone.

"Ole left it behind," she said. "You make the calls." She grabbed her cane and hurried up the hillside.

Daniel followed, dialling as he ran. He made the most important call first – to his parents. His mom would take over from there, getting the proper attention sent their way. She'd also make it to the scene quicker. Although she had only a basic emergency nurse's bag, she would have some idea of what to do. At the very least, she would be able to make Mr. Pederson comfortable until the ambulance came.

When Dr. Roost and Daniel arrived at Ole Pederson's side, his breathing was almost non-existent. Dr. Roost grabbed his wrist but found no pulse. She got down and placed her ear near his mouth to listen, then put her hand on his chest. It barely rose.

"You silly old fool," she whispered, tears in her eyes.

Daniel knelt down beside them, and stroked Mr. Pederson's hand.

"Please, Mr. Pederson, be all right," he pleaded.

Dr. Roost gently loosened Pederson's clothing to give him more air. Daniel balled his own jacket into a makeshift pillow. Pederson barely noticed, although his eyelids did flutter. Dr. Roost cradled Pederson's head in her arms.

"How are we going to explain what happened?" Daniel whispered.

"I guess you could say he got sick down at the dig and made it back this far before we found him," Mildred Roost suggested. "But how will we explain the mess you're in?"

Dr. Roost stared at Daniel's dishevelled appearance. His sneakers were caked with muck and his pant legs wet and muddy. Streaks of dirt ran across his face and into his hair.

"It did rain earlier this morning," said Daniel. "Maybe, I can just say I was doing some work around my hideout and I slipped and got all muddy."

"Sounds weak to me, but maybe no one will notice," said Dr, Roost. "Go hide Ole's equipment and overalls behind those rocks," she directed.

Daniel hesitated, not liking to leave Pederson's side, then ran to obey. He came back moments later to an unchanged scene. He pulled out his water bottle and Mr. Pederson's handkerchief. Gently he cleaned his old friend's face. As he did so, Pederson opened his eyes. They were a murky grey, but they showed a spark of recognition. Pederson tried to speak, but the words caught in his throat.

Dr. Roost dabbed water on his lips and tilted his head to give him a sip. He rested for a moment with his eyes closed, and then he spoke. Daniel leaned closer to hear.

"Thanks for being my partner and friend, Daniel," Pederson murmured. "Wish I could be there to see the wonderful things you're going to do in your life."

"No!" Daniel wailed. "You're not going to die!"

"I want you to know, Daniel, that it has been an honour to know you these last couple of years of my life," Pederson whispered. "Before I met you, I was just a grumpy old man disillusioned with the scientific world and how they viewed my work. You made me feel worth-while again."

He paused to catch his breath and Daniel mopped his forehead. Then he continued, "It's meant a lot to me to watch you delight in the study of amazing prehistoric creatures. Thank you for helping me. I couldn't have wished for anything more if you'd have been my own grandson."

"But there's so much more we have to do, Mr. Pederson," Daniel felt his throat constrict. This couldn't be the last time he'd talk with Pederson.

"And you will be able to carry on magnificently," said Pederson. "You'll have our memories and our connection will always exist through your work in paleontology.

I predict great things for you, Daniel Bringham. It brings me great comfort to know that you will go on with the research."

Ole Pederson's eyes shifted to Dr. Roost. "I'm sorry I didn't take you on my last trip, Mildred." He paused and swallowed. "I didn't want to put your life in danger and I hoped you'd carry on my work."

Dr. Roost nodded as tears welled in her eyes. "I will," she said.

In that instant, Daniel knew for sure that there was more between the two old people than their passion for paleontology. They loved each other, and the sadness he felt knowing that was almost too much to bear. Neither he nor Dr. Roost could speak, as they strained to hear Pederson's words.

"Mildred, even though I know you're not lacking in anything, my shack and land are yours," he continued. "When you're done with them, I'd like them to go to Daniel."

Dr. Roost nodded and clung to Mr. Pederson's hand. "Take care of yourself and this brilliant young man, Mildred. You both have much to accomplish."

A sob escaped from Daniel. "Please, Mr. Pederson, hang on," he pleaded.

"Daniel, I've had a great life, made all the better because of you." Pederson gazed lovingly at him.

"But, if I'd never taken you back in time, you'd be fine now," Daniel's words caught in his throat.

"Don't ever blame yourself for my dying." Pederson looked at him earnestly, "I *chose* to go back again; I was going to die soon anyway. Seeing the prehistoric world has been an incredible thrill at the end of my very long life. You've helped a lonely old man find much happiness. Always remember that."

"I will," said Daniel, letting the tears slide down his face.

"Bye, Mildred." Pederson closed his eyes.

"I won't be long behind you," she whispered, still gripping Pederson's hand.

"Bye, Daniel." Pederson never spoke again.

Daniel laid his head on Pederson's chest and wept. Mildred sat with an arm around each of them, looking out over the prairie.

Sometime later Daniel felt Dad's comforting arms lifting him away from Mr. Pederson. Through blurry eyes, he saw Mom bend over the old man, and shake her head. The ambulance people and others arrived. They lifted Mr. Pederson's body onto a stretcher and then he was gone. Daniel felt numb and hardly noticed as Mom guided him down the hill towards their truck. He sensed rather than saw that Mildred Roost lingered behind.

Daniel resisted them, and pointed to the shack. "I'd like to stay here for a bit. I'll come home in a while."

Mom nodded in understanding and hugged him. Dad hugged him briefly too and let him go with a quick shoulder squeeze. Daniel stumbled over to the shack and leaned heavily against an outer wall. As he slid down to sit on the ground, he heard the vehicles leaving, including Dr. Roost's truck, but he stared blankly at the landscape. Dactyl came over and licked at the wetness on his face. He pushed his head under Daniel's arm and laid his head on his lap. Absent-mindedly, Daniel stroked his dog's head.

Gradually details of his surroundings came into focus, as the sun dried the salty tears on Daniel's face. The little white crosses indicating places to dig for possible fossils; another for the gravesite of Pederson's dog, Bear; and the one in honour of his wife's last resting place. Daniel's thoughts touched on the memories he'd shared with Ole Pederson – of their first meeting at Daniel's hillside hide-out, their happiness at working together on Pederson's *Edmontosaurus* discovery, their involvement in paleon-tology and the tours, and the wonder and amazement of Pederson's first excursion into prehistoric time.

A deep sadness engulfed him, leaving him totally empty and hollow. He couldn't believe his friend was gone, that he'd never speak with him again. He glanced at the door, half expecting him to walk out, join him and discuss their latest adventures.

What would Daniel do without him? What would become of the work they'd done so far?

A small spark flashed in Daniel's brain. He'd have to make sure Pederson got the proper recognition for all his discoveries. Maybe they could name the *Stygimoloch* after him. Daniel shifted and Dactyl moved off him. Time to get home and find out what was going on. First, though, he had to retrieve his backpack and Mr. Pederson's gear. Luckily, the stuff was on the way home.

Daniel walked up the hill, scouring the surroundings, but someone must have taken everything. Their gear was gone. He had to get to it fast. He knew for sure that neither he nor Mr. Pederson had brought back any more prehistoric material that could be accidentally picked up, but he didn't want anyone to see the contents and the surprise of his or her life!

Daniel jogged across the pasture in a daze and made it home a few minutes later to find the yard filling with vehicles. Already the news about Ole Pederson had spread and neighbours had come to offer condolences and support. They milled about the yard, chatting quietly, gathered mostly by the outdoor kitchen, where Greta Lindstrom had set up a huge coffee urn. Mom saw Daniel and met him near the shop.

Tears sprang into his eyes again at the sympathetic look Mom gave him. She hugged him as he gulped back his sorrow.

"Go into the house if you like," she suggested. "You don't need to stay with the others."

He swiped tears off his face. "No, I'm fine. I'd rather be out here."

"Okay," Mom said, tousling his hair.

Numbly, Daniel walked through the crowd accepting sympathy. He wandered over to Dr. Roost's truck, hoping to find her there. She opened her camper door and stepped out, even before he arrived.

"I saw you were back," she said. She avoided looking into his eyes. She seemed to know he was on the verge of crying again and didn't mention Mr. Pederson.

"Do you know where our gear is?" he asked when he felt he could talk without breaking down.

"I have it safely here." She motioned to the front seat of the truck. "Didn't want it falling into the wrong hands. Get it whenever you want."

He nodded with a tight smile of thanks. There was no hurry to go through anything. They leaned against Dr. Roost's truck, watching as more vehicles arrived. Then Daniel spotted Corporal Fraser coming their way. When he offered his condolences, Daniel nodded thanks, then looked away to keep control of his emotions. A moment later, Dr. Roost stiffened beside him.

"What is it?" he asked.

"Newspaper time," she answered.

"Not that Adrian McDermott again!" Daniel said.

"No. It's Mr. Digby, the owner. Probably wants the info for Ole's obituary," she said.

"They sure don't waste any time!" he said. "I wonder what's happened to Adrian McDermott."

Mildred Roost shrugged. "Probably not exciting enough for him to cover."

Corporal Fraser had reached them and overheard Mildred's remark. "Well actually, Mr. McDermott won't be gathering news for the community any more."

Dr. Roost and Daniel turned their full attention towards the officer.

"Turns out he and two of his buddies from Swift Current were the ones that stole the *Stygimoloch* from you," Corporal Fraser said.

"Really?" Daniel asked, eyes widening. He'd always suspected Horace Nelwin. What shocked him was Adrian McDermott's involvement. "But why did he do it?"

"Seems there wasn't much news going on around here and he decided to create a sensational story of his own," said Corporal Fraser.

"So, he's one of those ambitious sorts, who wanted something that would garner him national attention and further his career," Mildred Roost added with a touch of scorn.

"What a terrible thing to do!" Daniel exclaimed.

"Yes. And what's worse," said Corporal Fraser, "he was going to wait a while and then pretend to find the fossils."

"Making out like he was some kind of a hero, I suppose," Dr. Roost said.

Corporal Fraser nodded.

"How did he even know about the fossils?" asked Daniel.

"Horace Nelwin spouted off about the special fossil find in the bar one night," he said. "When Horace went missing, McDermott lied about him going to Maple Creek to throw suspicion on him."

"I figured he'd actually done it," said Daniel.

"No, he only set things in motion," said Corporal Fraser.

"Todd told him, didn't he? I knew he was involved somehow!" Daniel couldn't keep the anger out of his voice. He stepped forward and scanned the yard looking for the Nelwin brothers.

"Not so fast," Corporal Fraser said. "Apparently Horace overheard his sons talking about it one morning when they were doing chores at home. When Todd heard of the theft, he worried that his Dad had been listening. He was scared about what would happen to his dad and scared for his brother and himself."

"So that's why he's been behaving so strangely," said Dr. Roost.

Daniel's anger over Todd's blunder dissolved. He'd been wrong about Todd.

"But how did you know it was McDermott?" asked Daniel.

Corporal Fraser smiled. "As soon as you told me his source was listening to the police band on the Internet, I knew he was lying. Our calls aren't transmitted that way."

"So that's why you doubled back at the old shack," Daniel said.

"That's right," said the corporal. "I figured he'd show up."

"Good thing you did too," said Dr. Roost.

"I see your dad is asking people to leave," said Corporal Fraser. "I'll see if I can give him a hand and then I'll be on my way."

The corporal took a few steps away before Daniel suddenly remembered something he wanted to ask.

"Did you ever figure out who dumped the oil barrel?" Daniel called after him.

Corporal Fraser said, "It seems Horace Nelwin isn't completely innocent in that event either. He was hauling used oil to be disposed of, but when one barrel fell off, he didn't worry about it."

"He probably didn't even notice it happen," said Dr. Roost with a snort.

"That's his defence," Corporal Fraser said. He wished them well and moved away.

Daniel frowned. "Horace Nelwin has caused a lot of problems."

"Indeed," said Dr. Roost. "The man's a walking source of trouble. He's certainly caused us a lot of grief over the *Stygimoloch*, that's for sure."

"Because of Todd!" Daniel's anger flared up again and he wanted to lash out at him. If only Todd had spoken up sooner, Daniel would never have encouraged Pederson to take a trip into the past and his old friend would be alive.

Dr. Roost came up quietly beside Daniel. "Don't blame anyone for this," she said, with her eerie way of knowing what he was thinking.

She put her arm around Daniel's shoulder. "Ole Pederson would have found a way to go anyway. He always knew you had something to transport you back to prehistoric time and he was determined to get there. You gave him the most incredible gift of his entire life."

Mildred Roost squeezed Daniel tight. "He died carrying out his passion for research in paleontology. Don't ever doubt that or blame yourself or anyone for his death. He would never have passed up the opportunity to experience what other humans will never know."

Quietly Daniel said, "If only he'd seen your note. That might have stopped him from going the last time. I wonder what happened to the note."

Dr. Roost pulled a scrap of paper out of her pants pocket. "Part of it's here," she said. "I found it trampled on the ground. The breeze or something must have knocked it off the peg on the door."

"You're not to blame either," said Daniel, knowing how devastated she must feel.

Her eyes held a deep sadness. "You're right. He's gone, Daniel. There's no going back, only moving forward."

She patted his hand. "I'll miss him."

She turned heavily and entered her camper.

Daniel stared after her, until he heard his name called. He turned to find Dad beckoning. He met him midway across the yard.

"Everyone's almost gone," Dad said. "Let's go in the house where it's quiet. We have a lot to think and talk about." Dad put his arm around Daniel's shoulders. "Especially now that the bank said we could keep on going with the tourist operation."

"They did?" Daniel looked at his dad in surprise.

"Yes, they phoned just before we got your call about Ole Pederson," said Dad. "But I'm not sure what we'll do now that he's gone."

Daniel suddenly remembered Mr. Pederson's bequest to Mildred Roost. "I think Dr. Roost might be convinced to stay on."

"That would be great," said Dad. "We'll talk to her after things have settled down a little and we've paid our respects to Mr. Pederson."

Daniel told his dad about the last conversation he'd had with Pederson before he died.

"That was very generous of him," said Dad.

Daniel nodded. "I still can't believe he's gone."

"It'll take some time to get over the shock," Dad said.

"I don't think I'll ever get over missing him," replied Daniel, feeling close to tears again.

"Come on, let's get you inside," Dad said.

But Daniel noticed Todd and Craig heading their way. "I'll be there in a minute," he said, indicating the Nelwin brothers.

Dad nodded and headed to the house.

When they reached him, the brothers murmured their condolences.

"We're sure going to miss him," said Craig. His eyes were shiny with held back tears.

"Yeah, he was an awesome person," Todd added, his

expression sombre, his face blotchy red. "He saw the good in everyone."

Daniel glanced at Todd, feeling a jolt of guilt. "Unlike me," he said.

"Yeah, I thought you suspected I was involved in the theft," said Todd.

"You were acting pretty suspicious," Daniel said in self-defence. "You took off right after it happened."

"I suppose that's the way it might have looked," said Todd. "But you know I've changed. You should have trusted me."

Daniel hung his head for a moment and then looked back up at Todd. "You're right. I apologize." Daniel spoke quietly. "I hope we can still be friends."

Todd stared at Daniel for a split second and then nodded. "Yeah, I'd like that." He reached out and shook Daniel's hand. "But next time, just ask." Although his voice was as gruff as usual, his face held a hint of a smile.

"Okay," Daniel said, smiling back.

"Good," said Craig, breaking into a relieved chuckle. "Well, I guess we'd better get home. We'll come back later to help you with the chores, if that's okay?"

Daniel smiled. "Yeah, I'd like that," he said.

As they turned to go, Daniel said, "Uh, just one more thing. I was wondering if I could ask you something. It's kind of personal, so you don't have to answer."

The boys looked at him expectantly.

"Go ahead," said Todd at last.

"So where was your dad, anyway?"

Todd grimaced, a little embarrassed. "He was over with one of his bachelor drinking buddies on a longer binge than usual. He just lost track of time."

"At least that mystery is solved," said Daniel. "Thanks for telling me."

All at once, Dr. Roost emerged from her truck camper and called to them. When they walked over to her, Daniel could see her eyes were red-rimmed and her face flushed and reddened.

"Boys, how would you like to go out prospecting Saturday morning?"

Surprised, they looked at one another, not sure what to say.

With a small smile, Daniel said, "Yes, I'd like to do that. I'm sure that's what Mr. Pederson would have wanted us to do."

"I say yes too," said Craig.

"Count me in," added Todd, shuffling his feet. There was silence for a moment and then he added, "I'm sure going to miss him."

"We all are," said Dr. Roost. "But I think this will be a nice way to remember him."

"I do too," said Daniel.

The brothers agreed.

"Okay, then, see you Saturday morning after chores," said Dr. Roost, before returning to her truck.

A moment later, she called back, "Oh, and see if Jed and Lucy or anyone else wants to come too. Everyone's welcome. We'll walk to the quarry and start from there. Maybe everyone should bring a lunch so we can make a day of it."

Craig and Todd left then and Daniel took the opportunity to grab the backpacks from Dr. Roost's truck.

After he'd safely stowed them in his bedroom, he examined his clothing and other gear to make sure there were no remnants attached anywhere from prehistoric time. He doubted he would ever have found the courage to go on another adventure to the Cretaceous Period, and he was relieved that nothing was left and he had absolutely no way to go again.

He stared out of his bedroom window across the pasture, drying under the autumn sun. Recollections of Ole Pederson and the times they shared flooded into his mind. For a brief moment, when the clouds obscured the sun and cast shadows over the landscape, he thought he saw his special friend striding across the hills. Then he was gone.

Daniel knew he would never let the memory of Ole Pederson or his work die. Every time he found a fossil or did any paleontology work, he'd remember him and their amazing connection. That meant he'd be thinking about Mr. Pederson a lot, because Daniel was sure there were plenty of other fascinating fossils buried in the surrounding hilly countryside. He would use the knowledge and wisdom Mr. Pederson had taught him and follow his guiding hand to find something spectacular that would have made his old friend proud.

VOCABULARY/DESCRIPTIONS

The material about paleontology found throughout this novel comes mostly from the Cretaceous Period. A brief description of some of the terms used follows, with their pronunciations. The Frenchman River Valley, where this story takes place, is located in the southwest area of Saskatchewan.

TERMS

CRETACEOUS PERIOD *(cree-TAY-shus):*
The Cretaceous Period, 146 to 65 million years ago, was the latter part of the Mesozoic era when great dinosaurs roamed the land and huge flying reptiles ruled the skies. A variety of smaller mammals and creatures also populated the earth and seas. The world was one of tropical temperatures all year round. Flowering plants and trees made their first widespread appearance, creating bright, beautiful places with their reds, yellows, and purples. Before that time, there were only the browns and greens of trees and ferns and the blues of the skies and seas.

NOTE: *Creta is the Latin word for chalk. The Cretaceous Period is named for the chalky rock from southeastern England that was the first Cretaceous Period sediment studied.*

GLOBAL WARMING:

Global warming is the term used to describe the increase in the average temperature of the earth's near-surface air in recent decades and its projected continuation. This is caused by trapping too much of the greenhouse gases in the atmosphere.

GREENHOUSE EFFECT:

The greenhouse effect was first discovered in 1824 by Joseph Fournier and studied more fully in 1896 by Svante Arrhenius. It is the process in which emissions of infrared radiation warm a planet's surface. Infrared radiation occurs when the sunlight creates energy or heat and it is reflected back into space. The greenhouse effect occurs when some of these emissions are trapped by greenhouse gases.

GREENHOUSE GASES:

These are a group of gases in the atmosphere that help stop the sun's infrared radiation (heat) from escaping into space, which is called the greenhouse effect. Some of these greenhouses gases are necessary to keep the earth warm enough to live on.

There are two major types of greenhouse gases. Those that occur naturally and those which result from gases emitted as a result of human activities. When too much of the man-made greenhouse gases are unable to escape to space, this causes global warming.

IRIDIUM:

Iridium is a rare element on earth, but is found abundantly in meteors. Deposits of iridium left in craters have helped to identify the gouges as made by meteors hitting the earth.

K-T MASS EXTINCTION:

K-T stands for Cretaceous-Tertiary. "K" is for Kreide – a German word meaning chalk, the sediment layer from that time. "T" is for Tertiary, the geological period that followed the Cretaceous Period. About 65 million years ago, it is believed that all land animals over 25 kg (55 pounds) went extinct, as well as many smaller organisms. This included the obliteration of the dinosaurs, pterosaurs, large sea creatures like the plesiosaurs and mosasaurs, as well as ammonites, some bird families, and various fishes and other marine species. There are many theories as to why this mass extinction occurred, but many scientists favour the one of an extraterrestrial body, a meteor, or asteroid hitting the earth.

During the K-T extinction, it has been estimated that 80-90% of marine species, about 50% of the marine genera, and about 15% of the marine families went extinct. For land animals, about 85% of the species, about 25% of the families, and about 56% of the genera died out. Larger animals (over about 55 pounds = 25 kg) were all wiped out.

METEORITE CRATERS:

There are many meteorite craters all over the earth. Those over 100 km in diameter had significant effects on the extinction of the species. Some of the biggest craters include one in the Yucatan province of Mexico; the Barringer Meteorite Crater near Flagstaff, Arizona, and others in Australia, Europe and North America. In Canada there are several in Quebec and some in Ontario, Nova Scotia, Manitoba, Newfoundland and Saskatchewan. The most famous in Saskatchewan is the Carswell Crater by Cluff Lake in the northern part of the province.

PALENTOLOGY *(PAY-lee-on-TALL-o-gee):*

Paleontology is the branch of geology and biology that deals with the prehistoric forms of life through the study of plant and animal fossils.

PHYTOPLANKTON *(FEE-toe-PLANK-ton):*

Phytoplankton are minute, free-floating aquatic plants.

PHOTOSYNTHESIS *(FOE-toe-SIN-the-sis)* (photo=light, synthesis=putting together):

In order for plants to make food for themselves, they use a method called photosynthesis. The "green" part of the leaves (chlorophyll) captures light from the sun, using it to form a sugar along with carbon dioxide and water. Plants release oxygen as a by-product of photosynthesis.

TERTIARY PERIOD *(TUR-sheer-ee):*

The Tertiary Period is the name for a portion of the most recent geological era known as the Cenozoic era, also known as the "Age of Mammals," which lasted from about 65 to 2 million years ago. The term Tertiary was coined about the middle of the eighteenth century and refers to a particular layer of sedimentary deposits. Many mammals developed during that time, including primitive whales, rodents, pigs, cats, rhinos, and others familiar to us today.

VOLCANIC ACTIVITY:

Prehistoric volcanoes created dramatic changes in greenhouses gases and global warming of the earth. They raised sea temperatures and killed off many marine species. (See K-T Mass Extinction for details of species that died.) Today they are mostly found in the northern hemisphere, but in prehistoric time they were found in the south. They spewed deadly amounts of ash, pumice and carbon dioxide into the air.

CREATURES MENTIONED IN THE BOOK

ANKYLOSAURS *(AN-kye-loh-sawrs):*
A group of armoured, plant-eating dinosaurs that existed from the mid-Jurassic to the late Cretaceous Periods. *Ankylosaurus* was a huge armoured dinosaur, measuring about 7.5–10.7 m long, 1.8 m wide and 1.2 m tall; it weighed roughly 3–4 tonnes. Its entire top side was heavily protected from carnivores with thick, oval plates embedded (fused) in its leathery skin, two rows of spikes along its body, large horns that projected from the back of the head, and a clublike tail. It even had bony plates as protection for its eyes. Only its underbelly was unplated. Flipping it over was the only way to wound it.

BASILEMYS *(BAH-zil-emm-ees):*
A tortoise-like creature with a shell up to 1.5 metres across. This is the largest known fossil turtle from the Frenchman River Valley.

BOREALOSUCHUS *(BOR-ee-al-o-such-us):*
A crocodile in existence in the late Cretaceous Period in Saskatchewan. This crocodile would be little compared to its earlier ancestors, about two to three metres in length. It would be running from a *T. rex* as opposed to taking it head-on like the larger crocodiles.

CHAMPOSAURS *(CHAMP–oh–SAWRS):*
Most of the champosaurs are fairly small, reaching only about 1.5 meters in length, but some specimens over three meters (about 10 feet) in length have been recently found in North Dakota. They had long, narrow jaws with fine, pointed teeth, and closely resemble the modern gavial of India. They may look like crocodiles, but are not closely related to them. Champosaurs fed on fish, snails, mollusks, and turtles. They lived in Saskatchewan from about 75 million years ago to about 55 million years ago.

CIMOLOPTERTX *(sim–oh–LOP–ter–icks)* ("Cretaceous wing"):
An early bird resembling typical shorebirds of today and found in the late Cretaceous Period in Saskatchewan. These birds had long, slender bills and long, strong legs for wading and running. They probably probed in the sand or mud for food.

CORYTHOSAURUS *(co–RITH–oh–SAWR–us)* ("Helmet lizard"):
Corythosaurus was a large plant-eating duck-billed dinosaur that probably fed on palm leaves, pine needles, seeds, cycad ferns, twigs, magnolia leaves and fruit. It may have weighed up to 5 tonnes and was about 2 metres tall at the hips and 9 to 10 metres long. (NB: *Corythosaurus* are known from slightly older sediments.)

DROMAEOSAURUS *(DRO-mee-o-SAWR-us)* ("fast-running lizard"):

Dromaeosaurus was a small, fast, meat-eating, theropod dinosaur about with sickle-like toe claws, sharp teeth, and big eyes. It lived during the late Cretaceous Period and was about a half a metre tall at the hips and 1.8 m (6 feet) long, weighing roughly 15 kg. Fossils have been found in Alberta, Saskatchewan and Montana. They were very smart, deadly dinosaurs and may have hunted in packs.

EDMONTOSAURUS *(ed-MON-toh-SAWR-us)* ("Edmonton [rock formation] lizard"):

A large, plant-eating member of the duckbill dinosaurs, or hadrosaurs that lived about 73 to 65 million years ago in the Cretaceous Period in western North America. It had hundreds of teeth crowded together in the huge jaw, enabling it to eat tough leaves and other vegetation. This flat-headed duckbill grew to 13 metres and weighed 3.1 tonnes. It may have had anywhere from 800 to 1600 teeth. *Edmontosaurus Saskatchewanensis*, named in 1926 by Sternberg, is the only identified species of *Edmontosaurus* so far known from Saskatchewan.

GARFISH *(A.S. gar, "spear"):*

Garfish is a name commonly given to certain fishes with long, narrow bodies and bony, sharp-toothed beaks. Primarily freshwater fish, today the largest tropical gar reach lengths of 3.7 metres. They are a primitive fish that have existed for millions of years. They have needlelike teeth, a dorsal fin that sits far back on the heavily scaled body. They are able to breathe in stagnant water, and their roe is poisonous to many animals, including humans.

HADROSAURS *(HAD-roh-SAWRS)* ("bulky lizards"):
Hadrosaurs were a family of duck-billed dinosaurs that ranged from seven to ten metres long and lived in the late Cretaceous Period. They appear to have been highly social creatures, laying eggs in nests communally. Nests with eggs have been found in both Alberta and Montana. The only known hadrosaur in Saskatchewan is the *Edmontosaurus Saskatchewanensis* (see description above).

HESPERONIS *(HES-per-OR-nis)* ("western bird"):
Hesperornithids were a family of large flightless birds that swam in the oceans of the late Cretaceous and preyed on small fish. It has been found in the Upper Cretaceous of Western Kansas and Saskatchewan. It is likely that they swam and fed much like modern penguins. They were also apparently limited to the Northern Hemisphere, much like penguins are limited to the Southern Hemisphere today.

ICHTHYORNIS *(ik-thee-ORN-is)* (meaning "fish bird"):
Ichthyornis were toothed, tern-like birds, with large beaks and heads, dating from the Cretaceous Period. Although only about 20 cm long, they were powerful flyers and the

oldest-known birds to a keeled breastbone (sternum) similar to modern birds. It lived in flocks nesting on shorelines, and hunted for fish over the seas. Fossils have been found in Kansas and Texas and Alberta,.

MOSASAURS *(MOES-ah-SAWRS):*
Mosasaurs were a group of giant, lizard-like marine reptiles that extended 12.5 to 17.6 metres long. They were not dinosaurs, but may be related to snakes and monitor lizards. They were powerful swimmers, adapted to living in shallow seas. These carnivores (meat-eaters) still breathed air. A short-lived line of reptiles, they became extinct during the K-T extinction, 65 million years ago.

PTERANODONS *(tair-AH-no-dons):*
Pteranodons were large members of the pterosaur family from the Cretaceous Period. They were flying prehistoric reptiles, not dinosaurs, toothless hunters who scooped up fish from the seas. About 1.8 m long, they had a 7.8 m wing-span.

PTERODACTYLUS *(ter-oh-DAK-til-us)* ("winged finger"):
A flying, prehistoric reptile was a member of the pterosaurs group, with a wingspan that spread up to .75 metres. The wing was made up of skin stretched along the body between the hind limb and a very long fourth digit of the forelimb. They lived during the late Jurassic period.

PTEROSAURS *(TER-o-SAWRS)* ("winged lizards"):
Flying reptiles that included Pteranodons and Pterodactylus, they were the largest vertebrates ever known to fly. They lived from the Jurassic to the Cretaceous Period.

PURGATORIUS *(pur-go-TOR-ee-us):*
A small, rodent-sized mammal from the Cretaceous Period, they may have been about ten centimetres long and probably weighed no more than 20 grams. They fed on insects. Some have suggested that this mammal may have been the earliest primate known.

"SCOTTY":
Scotty is the *Tyrannosaurus rex* discovered in 1991 near Eastend, Saskatchewan by a schoolteacher. Surrounded by cement-like ironstone and sandstone, it was not unearthed until 1994–95 and was found to be one of the most complete *T. rex* skeletons of only twelve such discoveries in the world. At this time, the first coprolite – or fossilized dung – that can be attributed to a *T. rex* was also found.

STEGOCERAS *(STEG-oh-CEER-us)* ("roofed horn"):
A bipedal, herbivorous, dome-headed, plant-eating dinosaur from the late Cretaceous Period about 76 to 65 million years ago. The *Stegoceras* was about two metres long and lived in what is now Alberta. Its large head

housed a thick skull, a relatively large brain, and large eyes. Its skull was about 8 centimetres thick. Males had thicker domes than females, and older Stegoceras had thicker domes than younger ones. Stegoceras had a fringe of horny knobs along the rear of its skull. It had short forelimbs and a large, stiff tail. Stegoceras grew to be about 2.1 metres long and 1.2 metres tall. This plant-eater weighed roughly 78 kilograms. *(Not to be confused with a Stegosaurus [pronounced STEG-oh-SAWR-us], meaning "roof lizard," a plant-eating dinosaur with armoured plates along its back and tall spikes that lived during the Jurassic Period, about 156 to 150 million years ago.)*

STYGIMOLOCH *(STIJ-eh-MOLL-uk)* ("thorny devil" or "demon from the River Styx"):
This unusual-looking plant-eating dinosaur lived in the woodlands. It had a domed head with bumps on its skull, which was rimmed with many bony spikes up to 100 mm long. It was about 3 metres long, and weighed about 50–75 kg. This pachycphalosaurid dinosaur lived during the very late Cretaceous period, about 68 million–65 million years ago. Only parts of *Stygimoloch's* skull have been found in Montana and Wyoming and in Alberta. The *Stygimoloch* was named after the River Styx of Greek mythology and because it was found near Hell Creek.

THESCELOSAURUS *(THES-ke-loh-SAWR-us)* ("Marvellous lizard"):

This plant-eating dinosaur had a small head, a bulky body that was 3–4 metres long, and less than one metre tall at the hips. A member of the ceratopsian group, it also had a long, pointed tail and shorter arms and could probably run at about 50 km/hr for an extended time. Two partial skeletons have been found in Saskatchewan.

TOROSAURUS *(TOR-oh-SAW-rus)* ("pierced lizard"):

Torosaurus had a strong toothless beak that was able to handle the toughest vegetation including small branches. A member of the ceratopsian group, it had a fierce appearance due to the two brow horns on its enormous 2.5 metre skull, a short nose horn, and a long-frilled crest. Its powerful legs were shorter at the front and longer at the back, which gave it a very stable posture. *Torosaurus* could chew well with its cheek teeth. They lived about 70–65 million years ago, and fossils have been found in the United States in Wyoming, Montana, Colorado, South Dakota, New Mexico, Texas, Utah and in Canada in Saskatchewan.

TRICERATOPS *(tri–SER–uh–tops):*

Triceratops was a rhinoceros-like dinosaur with a bony neck frill that lived about 72 to 65 million years ago. From the ceratopsian group, this plant-eater was about 8 metres long, 3 metres tall, and weighed from 6–12 tonnes. A relatively slow dinosaur, it had had three horns on its head and its parrot-like beak held many cheek teeth and a set of powerful jaws. It had a short, pointed tail, a bulky body, column-like legs with hoof-like claws. Many *Triceratops* fossils have been found, mostly in the western United States an in western Canada, including Saskatchewan.

TROODON *(TROH-oh-don):*
A very smart, human-sized, meat-eating dinosaur from the late Cretaceous Period. Fossils of *Troodon* have been found in Montana, Wyoming, Alberta and Saskatchewan. It may have been one of the smartest dinosaurs, because it had a large brain compared to its body size.

TYRANNOSAURUS REX *(tye-RAN-oh-SAWR-us recks or Tie-ran-owe-saw-rus-recks)* ("tyrant lizard king"):
A huge, meat-eating theropod dinosaur from the late Cretaceous Period. The largest meat-eater that has ever been, it stood 5–7 metres tall on its great clawed feet and had terrible, dagger-like teeth, 15 centimetres long. *Tyrannosaurus rex* was roughly 5–7 tons in weight. The enormous skull was about 1.5 metres long. The eye sockets in the skull are 10.2 centimetres across; the eyeballs would have been about 7.6 centimetres in diameter.

ZAPSALIS *(ZAP-sa-lis)* ("through shears"):
A meat-eating dinosaur (a theropod) that lived during the Cretaceous Period. This theropod was found in the

Judith River Formation, Montana in 1876. It is only known through its teeth and is currently classified as a troodontid.

OTHER REFERENCES & NOTES

BEES:

Over the past few years, Stephen Hasiotic, a Colorado University doctoral student and geology lab instructor, has found nests, almost identical to modern honeybee nests, that date back 207 to 220 million years, or about twice as far back as the oldest fossils of flowering plants. This means bees have been around longer than previously thought. The ancient bees could have found sugars and nutrients – which they find today in the nectar of flowers – in coniferous plants or even in animal carcasses.

COPROLITE:

Coprolite – or fossilized dung – has been found in many areas, but the specimens found in 1994–95 with "Scotty" in the Frenchman River Valley was the first that could be officially be attributed to a *T. rex.* This was an important discovery as it provides insights into its environment and eating habits.

DRAGONFLIES:

Dragonflies, primitive flying insects that can hover in the air, evolved during the Mississippian Period, about 360 to 325 million years ago. Huge dragonflies with wingspans up to 70 centimetres existed during the Mesozoic Era (when the dinosaurs lived).

ENVIRONMENTAL SCIENTISTS:

Environmental scientists and hydrologists use their knowledge of the physical makeup and history of the Earth to protect the environment, study the properties of underground and surface waters, locate water and energy resources, predict water-related geologic hazards, and offer environmental site assessments and advice on indoor air quality and hazardous-waste-site remediation. *(Taken from: http://www.bls.gov/oco/ocos050.htm)*

BIBLIOGRAPHY

Bakker, Robert T., *Dinosaur Heresies*, Morrow, New York, 1986.

Gross, Renie, *Dinosaur Country: Unearthing the Badlands' Prehistoric Past*, Western Producer Prairie Books, 1985. ISBN: 0-88833-121-5

Lauber, Patricia & Henderson, Douglas, *Living with Dinosaurs*, Bradbury Press, New York, 1991. ISBN: 0-02-754521-0

MacMillan Illustrated Encyclopedia of Dinosaurs and Prehistoric Animals, Cox, Dr. Barry, Harrison, Dr. Colin, Savage, Dr. R.J.G., Gardiner, Dr. Brian, editors: MacMillan London Ltd., 1988.

McIver, Elisabeth E., "The Paleoenvironment of Tyrannosaurus rex from Southwestern Saskatchewan, Canada," NRC Research Press Web site at http://cjes.nrc.ca, 20 February, 2001. Reference: *Can. J. Earth Sci.* 39 (2002), Pages: 207–221

Norman, David, & Milner, Angela, *Dinosaur*, Dorling Kindersley Ltd., 1989. ISBN 0-7894-5808-x

Parker, Steve, *Dinosaurs and How They Lived*, Macmillan of Canada, 1988. ISBN: 0-7715-96832-4 (Window on the World series)

Reid, Monty, *The Last Great Dinosaurs: An Illustrated Guide to Alberta's Dinosaurs,* Red Deer College Press, Red Deer, Alberta, 1990. ISBN: 0-88995-055-5

Relf, Pat, *A Dinosaur Named Sue,* Scholastic Inc., 2002. ISBN: 0-439-09985-4

Simpson, George Gaylord, *The Dechronization of Sam Magruder*, St. Martin's Griffin, New York, 1996. ISBN: 0-312-15514-X

Smith, Alan, *Saskatchewan Birds*, Lone Pine Publishing, 2001. ISBN: 1-55105-304-7

Stewart, Janet, *The Dinosaurs: A New Discovery,* Hayes Publishing Ltd., Burlington, Ontario, 1989. ISBN: 0-88625-235-0.

Storer, Dr. John, *Geological History of Saskatchewan,* Saskatchewan Museum of Natural History, Government of Saskatchewan, 1989.

Tokaryk, Tim T., "Archaeology: Puzzles of the Past," *Blue Jay,* 52 (2), June, 1994.

Tokaryk, Tim T., "Palaeontology: Treasures on the Shelves," *Blue Jay,* 52 (3), September 1994.

Tokaryk, Tim T., & Bryant, Harold N., *The Fauna from the* Tyrannosaurus rex *Excavation, Frenchman Formation (Late Maastrichtian),* Saskatchewan, 2004. http://www. ir.gov.sk.ca then search "Tokaryk".

Tokaryk, Tim T., "Palaeontology News: Encounters with Monsters," *Saskatchewan Archaeological Society Newsletter,* February, 1991, Vol 12, Number 1.

Tokaryk, Tim T., "Palaeontology News: A Tale of Two Vertebrae,"*Saskatchewan Archaeological Society Newsletter,* April 1992, Vol 13, Number 2.

Tokaryk, Tim T., "Palaeontology News: Serendipity, Surprises and Monsters of the Deep," *Saskatchewan Archaeological Society Newsletter,* October, 1996, Vol 17, Number 5.

Tokaryk, Tim T., *Scotty's Dinosaur Delights,* 1995. Friends of the Museum, Eastend, Saskatchewan.

Tokaryk, Tim T., *Preliminary Review of the Non-Mammalian Vertebrates from the Frenchman Formation (Late Maastrichtian) of Saskatchewan.* IN: McKenzie-McAnally, L. (ed) 1997. Canadian Paleontology Conference Fields Trip Guidebook No 6. Upper Cretaceous and Tertiary Stratigraphy and Paleontology of Southern Saskatchewan. Geological Association of Canada.

Wallace, Joseph, *The Rise and Fall of the Dinosaur,* Michael Friedman Publishing Group, Inc., New York, N.Y., 1987. ISBN:0-8317-2368-8.

URLS

http://www.answers.com

http://cas.bellarmine.edu/tietjen/images/tropical_paradise_at_the_cretace.htm

http://www.dinocountry.com

http://www.dinodatabase.com/dinoclas08.asp

http://www.emc.maricopa.edu/faculty/farabee/BIOBK/BioBookPS.html

http://www.enchantedlearning.com

http://www.nps.gov/dino/dinos.htm

http://teacher.scholastic.com/researchtools/
articlearchives/dinos/general.htm

http://www.tiscali.co.uk/reference/dictionaries/animals/
data/m0049059.html

http://users.tellurian.com/rmarguls/d-genera.html

http://www.dinosauria.com/dml/genera.htm

http://www.enchantedlearning.com/subjects/dinosaurs/
dinoclassification/genera/a.shtml

http://www.enchantedlearning.com/subjects/dinosaurs/
dinoclassification/Families.shtml

http://library.thinkquest.org/C005824/FAQ.html

AUTHOR'S WEB SITE

http://www.judithsilverthorne.ca/

ACKNOWLEDGEMENTS

My profound thanks to Tim Tokaryk, Senior Technician with the Royal Saskatchewan Museum Fossil Research Station in Eastend, for sharing his wealth of information and looking over my attempts at trying to look like I know what I'm talking about in the world of paleontology. Any errors are solely mine. Thanks also to Wes Long, Heather Gibson, and the staff at the T. rex Discovery Centre for their assistance and enthusiasm.

I salute Corporal Jim Fraser with the RCMP for his valuable information and support in the areas of police work, and congratulate him on recently receiving his new rank of Corporal.

A special thanks to Modeste McKenzie for suggesting character names and helping with descriptions and research, to Susan McKenzie for reading my manuscript in its early stages and offering plot ideas. Thanks also to my parents Stan and Elaine Iles for their instant assistance with farming and other rural details. The enthusiasm of you all is inspiring and your contributions appreciated. Thanks to everyone who assisted in any way with the details of this book, which has made the writing of this book so much easier.

My heartfelt thanks goes to Barbara Sapergia for her valuable insights and perceptive editing that contributed to the final focus and polish of the manuscript and for her hard work and dedication in guiding me along. Thanks also to Nik, Duncan, Karen and Deborah, a fabulous publishing team that I treasure highly.

ABOUT THE AUTHOR

Judith Silverthorne is a multiple-award winning Regina-based writer. She is the author of six novels for young readers with Coteau books, including: *The Secret of Sentinel Rock, The Secret of the Stone House, Dinosaur Hideout, Dinosaur Breakout* and *Dinosaur Stakeout.*

Two of her novels for young readers have won the Saskatchewan Book Award for Children's Literature. Her titles have received the "Our Choice" designation from the Canadian Children's Book Centre, while her first book, *The Secret of Sentinel Rock,* was also nominated for the Geoffrey Bilson Award for Historical Writing for Young People.

As a freelance writer, she has written several hundred articles and columns for newspapers and magazines. During the last few years she has also worked as an editor, researcher, curator, scriptwriter, and a television documentary producer. She also writing workshops and film classes, and does extensive author presentations and workshops.

Judith Silverthorne has lived most of her life in Saskatchewan, in both urban and rural settings, and it is the source of much of her material. She has recently engaged in extensive travelling and teaching English to foreign students, but continues to write young readers' and adult fiction, historical non-fiction books and articles.